Praise for *The Puppet Triangle*

"This book should be required reading for all 10 - 14 year olds to help them embrace their individuality, accept their personal circumstances and recognize their strengths as they make life-threatening decisions. I know that I'll be putting a couple of copies in my Special Education classroom!"

Heather Pollock

Special Education Resource Teacher/Guidance Counsellor

Englehart High School, Englehart, Ontario

"I counsel many students, like Brock's character, who are dealing with the wish to be accepted, peer pressures and the struggle to make wise life choices while others are not. I hope that by reading this book, many "puppets" see themselves portrayed and that they use the supportive tools described in 'The Puppet Triangle' in order to cut their own strings. Can't wait to buy the book for our library at TDSS!"

Beverley J. Gordon

Guidance Counsellor

Timiskaming District Secondary School, New Liskeard, Ontario

"The Puppet Triangle goes well beyond a typical day in the life of a pre-teen. It is a wise and wonderful book...that deals with the turmoils facing our pre-teens today and how they handle them. Each chapter is packed with insightful situations and how one person chose to deal with them."

Brenda Lemaire

Child and Youth Worker

St. Andrew Elementary School

"Great book! Easy to read and I love the suspense. As I read, I could see the story playing like a movie. Because of the friendship that has developed between Brock and the older gentleman, I recommend The Puppet Triangle to all readers, young and old. This would be a good book to have in a school library. I can't wait for your next book!!"

Jeannine Morrison

Occupational Therapist

North Bay, Ontario

"The Puppet Triangle is a great book that should be included in any library. Students will learn that bullying can happen to anyone, no matter the age, and it is not acceptable. This book is a great example on how by having friends who are older or younger than you, you can learn from each other's experiences and even help each other through difficult situations."

Anonymous

Dennis + Retta
Love always
Theresa
2007

THE
PUPPET
TRIANGLE

T. M. Deschamps

PublishAmerica
Baltimore

First printing

At the specific preference of the author, PublishAmerica allowed this work to remain exactly as the author intended, verbatim, without editorial input.

ISBN: 1-4241-2153-1
PUBLISHED BY PUBLISHAMERICA, LLLP
www.publishamerica.com
Baltimore

Printed in the United States of America

Dedicated to
Randy, Arissa-Lynn, Cody, Trenton and Brooklyn.

Special thanks to
Kevin McColley and Teri Martini
for making a dream true!

1

THE NIGHT HAWKS

A sad boy dropped his head. His chin reached his chest, but his heart dropped all the way to his shoes. "I wish you didn't have to go, Trenton. The summer is going to be long without you."

"It's only until Labor Day weekend, Brock. You have a full-time job at the garage and time will fly by. Besides, you're the lucky one, you even get paid for working."

Yeah, right, Brock thought. I'm the lucky one. "I feel like I'm losing someone again. I thought I was ready for the holidays, but I'm not."

A heavy framed boy pushed his glasses back on his nose. Trenton patted Brock on the back. "Listen to me. You will get through the summer just fine. I will call every week to see what you're up to. Bet you won't miss me at all."

Brock glanced down the driveway. He sighed. "I had plans to build birdhouses with my grandfather and now he is gone. I miss having our chats." He lowered his head and continued, "I haven't heard from my mom since my parents divorced. Seems like no one cares about me."

Trenton scuffed his old joggers along the pavement towards the family jeep. He twisted on the spot. "I'm coming back. I'll be home before you know it." The chubby boy hesitated. "It's not your fault your grandpa died. Your parents' divorce had nothing to do with you, Brock. You said yourself that your parents fought for months before they separated."

Brock slid his hands into tight jean pockets. "You are leaving for two months, my dad works all the time at the garage, and now I'm abandoned for the final time."

"Nobody's abandoning anyone, Brock. Snap out of it. Things happen in life and you have to change or adapt to the situation."

"Change or adapt?" Brock rubbed his chin. He had a brain wave! "That's it."

"What's it?"

"I can change into a whole new person. No more being the quiet guy or the stupid kid from special education class. No more being pushed around and laughed at by other students."

Trenton motioned to leave but swung around with saucer like eyes. "What are you talking about?"

Brock grabbed his friend's arm. "Your parents won't wait much longer. I'll see you Labor Day Weekend."

The chubby boy threw up his hands, "I'm not leaving until you tell me what crazy nonsense is going on in your head. You aren't planning something stupid, are you?"

"I don't need my mom, grandpa, dad or you to have a great summer." Brock rubbed his hands together while forming plans.

"This is not like you. I only mentioned you change or adapt to your personal circumstances. Turning into a complete stranger spells trouble."

"Whatever gave you the idea I'd be a stranger? Remember,

I'm shy! How can I become someone I'm not? What trouble can I possibly get into with nobody around? Go ahead and enjoy your visit in Wigston. Your grandparents will be happy to have you help out on the farm."

"No one mentioned getting into trouble, Brock. Your change of heart is totally out of your character. I don't want you doing something you'll regret."

A weakened posture transformed into a confident stroll as Brock walked Trenton to the road.

A bare and lonely street emerged in the west end of Northshore, a small town in northern Ontario. Twelve-year-old Brock Statler waved goodbye from the end of his driveway to his best friend as the red jeep drove out of sight. Distance grew between the boys as the vehicle turned the corner.

The first day of summer holidays began without his friend. Trenton left for eight weeks of fun and adventure on his grandparent's farm. Brock's summer alone emerged into the most difficult challenge he would have only imagined in his dreams.

Other classmates had exciting plans before Junior High school started in the fall. Grade seven was a new beginning for teens compared to boring elementary school. Junior High school meant no more young kids bothering you or following childish rules. Hanging out with older students over the summer developed maturity. The social scene prepared teens for first semester by new contacts made in advance.

Brock sat on the wooden steps outside his small bungalow home. He hugged his bony knees with slender arms, cradling his face between two kneecaps. His mind switched into overdrive as he prepared his big challenge.

Brock's dad was head mechanic downtown at Wilson's Auto Garage. Tuesday morning promoted him to mechanic's helper for summer employment. He looked forward to his first paying job and working with his father. He dreamed of becoming a mechanic like his dad. His new job would help reach his goal knowing he had one of the best teachers in town. Brock was determined to learn everything possible. Quality time spent with his dad was a bonus knowing they were together.

Brock's parents had divorced five years ago. He spent weekends at the garage and enjoyed being greased from head to toe. He loved working around dirty vehicles and the hoist fascinated him. His mother came to mind many times as he remembered telling her about his trips to the garage. He missed her hearty laugh and gentle ways. He wished for the warmth of slender arms wrapped tight to protect him from the outside world.

Raised by a single parent and being an only child had its advantages. Brock had a great relationship with his dad and enjoyed doing guy things together. He worked on his go-cart, ate takeout food more than usual, and left dirty clothes scattered on the bedroom floor until laundry day. A downfall was a communication barrier between him and his father when discussing his parents' separation. He felt guilty and reluctant to open up with his father in this department and sought comfort from his grandfather. It was now between him and his father to work out discussions.

When Grandpa Statler lived with them, it had been triple the fun. He kept his grandfather company on weekends while his dad worked. Grandpa Statler taught him how to repair and paint lawn furniture. He made birdhouses and experimented with wood scraps. A new project was always in progress.

Brock reminded himself that he was daydreaming. Grandpa was gone. Last month was tragic, and now his best friend was gone, too. Brock had two choices: spend the entire summer working with his dad and sulking alone in his room the rest of the time or he could change his life for the better. He decided challenging himself to a complete makeover in pursuit of adventure. His transformation into a confident, outgoing, risk taking person required motivation into his new adventure. Brock decided being tagged as a loner no longer fit his description. He had a backbone like everyone else. Now was his chance to prove that he knew how to use it.

Brock looked out into space from his front steps. The weather network forecasted a scorcher that day. The noon sun warmed the top of his head as soothing chirps sang from the birch tree beside the house. Lack of rain caused brown patches on the front lawn.

Brock placed a small sprinkler in the middle of the yard. The metal contraption kept him in a daze. He waited for sprouting water but nothing happened. His unexpected soaking had to wait for Trenton's return. Brock crossed the yard to the tap mounted on the side of the house. The tap squeaked as it turned. Cold water swirled over the dry ground in tiny droplets.

Brock studied the rusted tin roofing extended across the driveway. He examined the carport as if for the first time. The bent roof protected his dad's old Ford truck and also kept the side entrance dry. Brock loved the ping-pong sounds the rain made against the surface at night. He moped under the carport, reaching the back yard.

Yellow straw replaced green grass. Brock faced more yard work. A small storage shed sat off to the right, alongside a mesh fence. He decided spending his first day of summer vacation puttering around while he planned initial steps to finding adventure.

The oversized tin shed off balanced the small back yard. A

rust tainted roof showed aging signs. Seams parted at the corners adding years of usage to the building. A hard jerk scraped the crooked door sideways along a metal runner. Shelves lined both outer walls. Boxes supported the back wall with odds and ends stored over the years. An old gas lawn mower sat in the middle of the shed. Fumes mixed with a warm musty scent. Brock squeezed between the lawn mower and shelving to reach the rear of the shed. He checked for anything interesting and spotted a birdhouse half finished on the middle shelf. It was the last project him and his grandfather had worked on together.

Wood scraps, paint cans, brushes, sandpaper and nails remained in their spot. Cobwebs covered everything. Brock passed the time straightening up the shed. He stuck his head out the door for fresh air. A sweet scent of roses in full boom came from the neighbor's direction. He returned to the job at hand.

A noise from the driveway startled him. He tripped over the lawn mower wheel. Braced against the handle, he grabbed onto the sliding door. Brock peered through the small opening in attempt to exit the storage shed.

A tall husky boy raced up the driveway, skidding along the pavement. It was Justin Galley. No one in sixth grade was brave enough to make him mad. Justin was nicknamed 'Zipper' but never referred to by that name in person.

Suspicion crossed Brock's mind. He wondered why Justin showed up at his house. He wasn't the type of person to associate with this boy. The Galleys were a well-to-do family and Justin had no problem choosing friends. A fabulous idea jolted Brock like a lightning bolt. Maybe his classmate introduced his first step to finding friendship. This offered a big gamble but worth the risk.

Long brown hair hung over Justin's shoulders. He dropped

the ten-speed bike on the ground. Authority pronounced in each step.

"Hey Statler! Doing some house cleaning?"

"No." Brock closed the shed door.

He waited for an explanation for his classmate's visit. Brock inched his way to the front yard keeping Justin in his side view. He eased to the front steps sitting on the top one.

Justin hovered over Brock by five inches and a good twenty pounds. He plunked his butt beside him, giving a crooked grin.

Brock felt tiny sitting next to the large figure. Silence broke with a quick movement. Justin thumped flat feet onto the ground. "What plans do you have for the summer holidays besides cleaning out sheds?"

"Working for my dad at Wilson's Auto Garage this summer. I'm looking for some excitement to pass time when I'm off work."

The voice took on more authority. "See you have the makings of a go-cart in the driveway. Do you know anything about building them?"

"Some. My friend and I started that one." Brock realized his project was on hold until Trenton returned.

"Rumor has it your friend is gone for the summer. My friends are busy, too. We can hang out together if you want?"

Pity crossed Justin's face, bringing out the loner in Brock. He only had one true friend and he wasn't a charity case, but company sounded great. His classmate showed up at the right time and must have been sent as a sign for Brock. If anyone knew about adventure it was Justin. "Sure."

Brock wondered how a person like Justin had so many friends. At school, he terrorized younger students and was the class troublemaker. The teacher had sent him to the principles office almost daily for disrupting class. Justin managed to have a couple of guys at his side all the time.

Brock felt important talking to his classmate like a friend. Shyness made communication difficult and his learning disability forced him into a group of his own. Justin's rough attitude frightened him along with his size but his conversation sparked possibilities for the perfect 'challenge'.

"Want to check out the go-cart I'm working on? Yard work can wait until later."

Brock shared a common interest with his classmate. Whatever reasons Justin had for hanging out with him were not important. Besides, what was the worst thing that could happen? When a big guy like Justin Galley wants to be friends, the only sensible answer is, "Sounds good."

Brock grabbed the old gray frame leaning against the house. His ten-speed wasn't fancy like Justin's but it was faithful. A few gears worked better than none and the brakes were dependable.

The two boys rode down Princeton Street turning onto Mackey Avenue. A right turn brought them a short distance down Baker Street, switching to Martin and turning onto Dalewood Crescent. Brock watched the bike ahead of him zigzag along the road. Justin jumped curbs, ran onto private lawns, and weaved in and out of parked vehicles. Grandpa Statler turned over in his grave at this sight. Brock stayed a distance behind in case of an emergency stop.

Dalewood Crescent was a new subdivision. Large brick homes, double-car garages, and landscaped yards highlighted the block. New vehicles parked in nine out of ten driveways. Justin pulled into his yard dropping his bike half way up the paved drive. Brock rode up to the double garage and leaned his bike against the wall.

Colorful flowerbeds surrounded the plush green carpet.

Different sized shrubs centered the back yard. Bushes closed in the large deck situated at the rear of the house. Patio stones beside the house led to a three-leveled deck. Brock imagined such a display in the "Homes and Gardens" magazine. He never viewed a real scene.

Brock followed Justin through a back entrance to the garage. Tools scattered the cement floor. Go-cart parts were everywhere. Wilson's Auto Garage was cleaner than this place but the smell of oil was the same.

Brock gasped. On the far side of the garage sat the most beautiful old model T-Ford he had ever seen. "That's a beauty!"

"My old man is saving that old thing for a retirement project. He figures he'll have lots of time to work on it then."

"What about the old man?" said a stern voice.

Brock moved away from the old Ford stumbling over a box of car parts. "Sorry, sir." He bent over the mess and gathered pieces into the cardboard box.

"Leave those parts where they are. You'll have prints engraved into them with your dirty hands."

Brock dashed for the go-cart. He faced the door to see who had spoken. A tall slim man stood inside the doorway. Silver streaks shone in the sunlight. His dark eyes held a significant glare.

"I asked you a question," repeated the man.

Justin stepped backwards and froze. His face turned white. Fists clenched at his sides. He lowered his head and mumbled, "I told Brock about your retirement project."

"Watch your mouth when referring to your father. Clean up this junk before the garage is condemned for health violations." Mr. Galley approached the door. "Wasting time on trash is a lazy man's hobby." His arms flew above his silver top and the

15

garage door slammed behind him. A wrench flew from Justin's hand crashing against the brick wall. "I wish he'd take an extended holiday out of the country." A strange odor sailed under Brock's nose. The scent of booze smelled like skunk. He was speechless. He noticed Justin step away from his father. He looked like he had seen a ghost. Grandpa Statler's funeral recalled a similar fright for Brock. Justin appeared as terrified as he felt during that day at Marvin's Funeral Home.

Justin's dark hair tossed over his left shoulder as he spun around. A four-inch scar stood out as pronounced as Edward Scissorhands' switchblade fingers did in the movie. Brock wondered how Edward coped every day having strangers pointing at his hands. The marking on Justin's face alerted the same reaction.

The scar ran down his friend's left cheek. Tiny bumps the size of pinholes outlined the edge resembling teeth on a zipper. The seam appeared tightly sewn and ripping apart with the slightest smile. The disfigured face gave Justin an appropriate nickname. Brock shivered. He never came close enough before to see the marking.

He lowered his head not knowing how to react. "Did I make your dad mad because I was near his car?"

"He is always on the rampage about something. He gets mad just looking at me." Justin focused on the gears lying at his feet.

Brock scuffed his joggers back and forth on the concrete floor, making marks in the dirt.

"Your dad doesn't seem interested in you building a go-cart, does he?"

"First of all, he's my step-father. Secondly, he thinks if you don't have an office job requiring brains like an accountant, then you're doing lazy man's work. School studies are what interest him. I'm supposed to graduate as a lawyer, or judge, or some other boring professional."

Brock paced. "Where are your buddies that hang out with you?"

"They have stuff to do. A few of them got jobs for the summer and a couple are gone for a few weeks." Justin picked up a set of ten-inch wheels. "What do you think? Pretty good shape for bargain hunting, eh?"

Brock looked closer. "I've been looking all over for wheels like this for the front end. I have twelve-inch wheels for the back, but I want a low rider effect in front."

Justin grinned. "Let me know what you need and we'll find it."

"It must be nice having connections."

"Hey, there are people wanting to help a good cause everywhere you turn." Justin moved around the frame fitting pieces.

Brock's interest escalated. This guy had a masterpiece in the works. He snooped around the semi-built go-cart, observing the original work. Known for a troublemaker around school Justin's creative side was impressive. "I see you enjoy being a grease monkey too." Brock pointed at his friend's grimy hands.

Justin tilted his head, wiping grease onto a soiled pair of jeans. "I do what makes me happy. Working with my hands is what I like."

Brock pointed at the assembled frame. "How did you come up with your plans?"

"Magazines. I have a monthly Go-Kart Magazine and I take ideas and put them together until they work. What about yours?"

Brock avoided that awful sight on Justin's face. He rubbed the tight wrapping on the steering wheel. "I have a stack of magazines from Go-Kart Plans and ideas out of a new book I bought on making your own yard kart. Trenton makes easy to follow blueprints and I do the physical work."

Curiosity blurted out. "What happened to your face?" Justin raised his head. Brock made contact with the same big brown eyes as Mr. Galley. Knives plunged into his heart. Justin stood like a giant. He rubbed his hands on a dirty rag hanging out of his back pocket. He stepped closer pointing his finger. The rattled voice chilled Brock's spine.

"Don't ever mention my face again."

Paralyzed, Brock waited for his wobbling legs to collapse. Fear consumed his fragile body. Horror surfaced as he connected with demon eyes. He stepped back. Anger surrounded him with time frozen. Brock jumped.

Justin stretched his arms, revealing an evil grin. "Want a drink?"

Too spooked to answer, Brock nodded. Sweat beads dampened the front of his blue T-shirt. He was having a sauna in the middle of Justin's garage. His throat blocked off saliva building in his mouth.

Justin pulled two soft drinks from a bar fridge standing in the corner of the garage. He handed one to Brock. "You have any other friends besides Trenton?"

Brock wiped his brow and swallowed a long cold drink of Root Beer. "No."

"Have you ever been in a gang before?"

Brock wasn't sure where this line of questioning led so he took precaution. "No."

A smirk crossed the larger boy's face. He rested his tall frame against a tool chest. "Seems a shame to waste the summer alone. You wanted excitement Statler and we need some adventure. Want to start our own gang?"

Excitement blocked out any existing shyness. Brock stabbed his finger against his chest, "Me! You want me to join a gang?"

Justin searched around the cluttered garage. "You see me talking to anybody else. Yes, Statler. You and me."

"Don't we need more people for a gang?"

"One, three, fifteen, it doesn't matter how many people. Operation is what counts. Trenton can join if he wants when he comes back."

"That's great! Wait until I tell him." Brock clenched his fists in cheers. "He won't believe this." Enthusiasm exploded. He grabbed a seat on the nearest wooden crate diving in for all details. "What do we do first?"

Minutes passed and the ringleader said, "We need a name. Any ideas?"

Brock was too excited to think of a name for their new gang. He found the adventure he hoped for, washing away a boring summer. Justin seemed neat and didn't act anything like he did at school. Changing his behavior seemed less of a challenge to Brock, after all.

Justin and Trenton were opposites but Brock found someone to share his time with and maybe enjoy a completely new experience. His answered prayer replaced emptiness with a new friend.

"No ideas, Statler?"

"I'm not sure what names are used for gangs." Brock shook his head. *Way to go Statler, now you sound like a nerd.* His face heated with embarrassment. "I mean, an appropriate name for our gang."

Justin scratched the top of his greasy hair and paced the hard surface. "I've got it. What about the Night Hawks?"

The choice surprised Brock. He hesitated. "I imagined a less forceful approach. Aren't names supposed to represent the purpose of a gang?"

"Yes. Don't you like the Night Hawks?"

Brock thought it was a strange name but agreed. "Great! What's next?"

"All gang members have to take a pledge called, the Code of Silence. This joins all members to one group. An oath swears that anything we do or say can never leave our lips. Everything is top secret. This way if one member fails, everyone goes down with him."

This sounded scary but Brock's hunger for adventure and suspense pulled him forward. His social life climbed into the spotlight drawing him closer to the Night Hawks. An opportunity arrived for him to come out of hiding from his learning disability and belong to something. A gang presented more thrills than working at Wilson's Garage.

Rules never entered Brock's mind. The gang's purpose was a mystery but he nodded in approval anyway.

Justin took a pen and scrap of paper from his dad's tool chest. He wrote something down.

"Okay. Raise your left hand and read what is on the paper."

Brock looked at the wrinkled piece of paper in Justin's hand. His skin turned clammy. Perspiring fingers took the paper. The words floated together and his legs weakened. Letters danced across the page making the first sentence impossible to focus on.

"What's the matter, Statler?"

"Nothing." Brock's voice quivered.

A loud laugh broke the silence. "I forgot! You're in that special education class. Miss Johnson hasn't taught you guys how to read yet."

The words stabbed Brock. Insecurity slid into his gut with no return. His membership had expired because he was a slow reader. His head lowered in shame.

"Repeat after me."

A deep sigh escaped along with a nervous cough. Brock faced his ringleader and held up his right hand. *"I solemnly swear to abide by the rules laid out before me. Cross my heart and if I disobey the devil takes me into his hands."*

"Okay Statler. We'll make it easy on you. I'll read the pledge and you repeat it."

All one hundred pounds trembled with pleasure. Honor rose as Brock repeated the Code of Silence.

"As a pledge to the Night Hawks, I take this Code of Silence. I will never reveal our activities to anyone. The silence will never be broken or I will pay the consequences. I promise to follow and obey the leader at all times. I give my word and seal my lips."

Justin ran his fingers across his wide lips in motion to close. Brock followed by touching his dry lips. The ceremony ended in a handshake. Brock surged with energy and felt great!

Justin checked his watch. The empty pop can clanged into the corner of the garage. "My mom heads to work in an hour, so I want to catch her for some money before she leaves for the hospital."

Brock disappeared outside behind his new friend. He picked up his bike as the garage door closed.

"Canada Day Parade is on Monday. Want to go?"

"Sure! When and where do you want to meet?"

A long arm waved overhead as Justin slipped through the back door. "Your place at 12:30 p.m. I'll initiate you then."

"What initiation?" No one was in sight when Brock replied.

The ceremony was over. The initiation had shocked Brock. Nothing was worse than initiations at Northshore Junior High

School. Grade seven students ran for safety the first week of school. Seniors played terrifying stunts and Brock sensed a similar bag of tricks planned by Justin.

Brock rode home in a daze. He ran into a parked car. The stinging scratch reminded him to pay attention for the rest of the ride home. The code of silence ritual played through his head. The message remained loud and clear even if he forgot some words. Membership in a gang swallowed all thoughts until his sworn oath sunk in.

A strange vibration squirmed inside of him. Out of nowhere the Night Hawks frightened Brock. On the other hand, was it Justin Galley he feared the most? Terrified by the unexplained, Brock sensed trouble. He discovered adventure the first day of holidays and that's what he wanted. Something crawled inside his stomach forcing him to quit while he was ahead. The Night Hawks boosted Brock into the lead for adventure and the greatest challenge in a lifetime. His loneliness pushed forward for escape.

2

THE INITIATION

Membership in the Night Hawks carried excitement through the weekend for Brock. His holidays looked encouraging. He thought a new friendship introduced sharing ideas on building go-carts, bike racing, and maybe learning some awesome bike jumps.

Justin was a normal guy in most ways. His anger and hostility showed more than most teenagers Brock knew, but appeared understandable after witnessing Mr. Galley's reaction on Friday. Justin expressed the same evil look as his father, making friendship hesitant for Brock. He anticipated a different relationship with Justin compared to the one he had with Trenton. After all, his plans focused on a new approach for excitement and his ringleader was sure to supply the details.

Monday morning arrived. Initiation approached with interest fading. Curiosity no longer existed. Brock feared the outcome of his final stage in membership with the Night Hawks. Something mysterious settled around his new companion. As the clock ticked so did Brock's thoughts. Justin's speedy buddy system was disturbing. The Statler motto was be prepared for anything but unexpected events caused him doubts.

Brock took his time getting ready. He cleaned his bedroom and placed the 'Code of Silence' safe inside the binder on his desk. A pocket-sized dictionary rested beside the binder. The resource came in handy for frequent misspelled words.

It was departure time. Canada Day Parade and the Santa Claus Parade were his annual favorites. Brock enjoyed the craftsmanship in building the floats. Cartoon characters displayed moving heads and arms. Many people worked numerous hours creating original ideas. Enthusiasm diminished the annual importance of the Canada Day Parade. Initiation clouded his spirit. Brock hated unforeseen events.

He entered the kitchen and paced a path over the floor. His dad startled him.

"Excited as usual about the parade, are you son? You are wearing out the color on the tiles."

Brock clued in and sat at the table. Slouched in the chair he tapped his fingers on the wooden surface. Taps grew into thumps. His dad's voice brought him back to reality.

"Anything wrong son?"

"No."

His father shifted his eyebrows up and down. He gave his famous, 'want to try again' look.

"I'm going to the parade with Justin Galley. He's picking me up soon."

"Isn't his mother a nurse at North Central Hospital? She looked after your grandfather when he had his heart attack."

Brock peeked through the kitchen curtains. "Could be his mom. She works at the hospital."

"Are you nervous about something? You seem jittery."

"I hate waiting for people."

"Have a butter tart while you're waiting. Fresh from Papa Rick's own kitchen."

"I thought I smelled raisins when I woke up. Think I'll pass on your baking for now, Dad. Leave some for when I get back." Brock took another glance out the window. He waved on his way out the door. "I'll wait outside for Justin."

A wide smile pronounced two dimples on his father's thin chin. "Don't trust my baking, eh?"

Brock had the easiest going father in all of Northshore. He talked to his dad about men things, social issues, hobbies, and sometimes nothing in particular. He confided in his dad more since his grandfather died but his mother remained a distant topic.

Brock shared ideas with his best friend about special education class, bullies, and go-cart plans. Trenton was behind the times and an old fashioned guy. New technology confused him. The 'New Millennium' had advanced the computer scene like a heat wave in the year 2000 and his friend steered away from computers. Growing change and knowledge continued and this year was no different. Trenton's safe cocoon sheltered him from the outside world. Brock coped with new learning techniques while his friend remained focused on the old ways.

He enjoyed Trenton's company because he acted like a twelve-year-old guy with no pressures in the world. His friend's safeness caused envy.

Brock took an interest in everything at school whether he disliked it or not. He concealed his poor reading and spelling skills to belong to a group. He knew Miss Johnson was well known for teaching students with learning disabilities and his classmates were not blind. Students teased him every day. Justin Galley topped his fan list.

Brock's father mentioned the trouble gangs had caused in

small towns. His father sat in on a council meeting proposing a committee handling gangs in Northshore.

Brock was confused. He joined the Night Hawks without considering future consequences. He had to deal with this issue on his own. His dad's view was crystal clear about gangs. It was his choice to be a member and any problems that occurred were up to him to solve.

Grandpa Statler always said, *"Son decisions are not easy. Time and patience bring results."*

Brock waited a couple of minutes. He grabbed his beat up bike by the handlebars and plunked his butt on the tattered black seat. He searched for signs of Justin.

The morning sun reflected off his dad's old green Ford sitting in the driveway. A clear blue sky disagreed with rain forecasted. Sweet smelling flowers drifted in the light breeze. Birds perched on the maple branches confirmed it was a beautiful day for a Canada Day Parade.

Brock rode up and down the driveway. On and off the road he ventured. Torn pieces sticking up on his seat made his buttocks sore even though he was used to it. He applied pressure to flatten them down. His watch confirmed that Justin was late. Heat generated from the pavement beneath his soles. He wasn't sure if he perspired because of the temperature or the waiting game.

Brock headed for the Galley's house. Justin must have overslept. He remembered the street where Justin lived but forgot which house. He turned onto Dalewood Crescent. His pace slowed checking each house along the way.

A beach ball bounced out in front of Brock. He dodged a small girl running to claim her ball. Dogs barked as children raced around their yards. Rich green lawns flowed even across the properties. Brock envisioned his spotted yard rolling in lumps.

Tricycles, wagons, and toys scattered the curbs. Parents shouted at children on the road. Brock paused alongside the curb after passing a few homes. He looked for a familiar connection to Justin's house. He wasn't sure of the address number.

Someone yelled from across the street. A loud bang turned neighbors to see. The sound appeared close but then it muffled. No one was in sight.

An angry voice shouted. A tall boy bounced through the front door across the street. The frame stumbled down the cement steps. The boy held onto his right arm and raced for the garage. It was Justin.

The door flew open again. A man held a baseball bat in the air. Clenched fists shook the wooden stick. The bat swung above the man's head as he yelled, "Get back here. You don't walk away from me when I'm talking to you."

Justin's father was furious. "Answer me."

Mr. Galley whacked the bat against the brick wall after no reply. He lost his balance, tripped over the doorstep and fell inside the house. He mumbled as he picked himself up and slammed the door.

Justin darted from the garage, full speed past Brock. His arm motioned to follow. At the end of the street, he slammed on the brakes. Brock caught up to his buddy at the corner pulling close beside the curb. He pretended nothing happened, but his trembling hands grabbed the handlebars for steadiness.

Justin rubbed his right arm and moaned. Anger rose for a second time in his big brown eyes. The fight between Justin and his father set off uneasy vibes for Brock. He played with a piece of torn electrical tape on his seat until it ripped. His fingers stuck together from the sticky tape and he rubbed his hands on his shorts trying to remove the glue. He looked at the ground instead of his friends piercing eyes. The scar was rough enough dealing with but his leader's eyes were unpredictable.

"Why did you come to my house? I was supposed to meet you."

Brock thought it was safer not answering. He waited out the silence until Justin erupted. Fists banged against the metal bars. Rage escaped through strange grunts. "I hate him. I wish he would leave for good."

The outburst puzzled Brock because Justin delivered himself as a strong and fearless person. He stood over his bike like a normal thirteen-year-old boy who was frightened to death. Brock changed the subject after noticing the blue packsack. "Why are you carrying a packsack?"

The leader straightened his posture. He removed kinky hair from his face with a shake of his head. "The tools of the trade are in here. They are required for your initiation. Let's go or we will be late."

Brock stalled. He hoped that whatever problems existed between Justin and his father weren't going to interfere with his initiation. The thought stirred a spinning motion in the pit of his stomach. He felt plans changing by the second. His unsettled breakfast confirmed trouble was brewing. He followed the ringleader two streets over, crossing Mackey Avenue. Weekend drivers honked at friends as they drove by. Fresh cut grass filled Brock's nostrils making him sniff towards the clean scent. He tagged along a path leading through a field on the other side of the road.

Marsh Pathway was a paved trail designed for bike riding, roller blading, and jogging. Teenagers kept off the main streets and reported bike accidents declined with use of the trail. Railway tracks ran a few meters away. Oil drifted from the stained railway ties. The tracks branched off to the downtown area. Marsh Pathway ran close to Main Street where the parade began.

The boys crossed Freemont Street and into the midst of marching bands already in progress. People crowded both sides of the street. Brock watched for clues, but nothing warned him about his initiation. He considered calling it quits and going home, until beady brown eyes reminded him of Justin's temper. Maybe he over reacted, torturing himself for nothing. Justin might have planned a fun event, he thought. Curiosity pushed him onward watching every object with caution.

Justin pulled into a vacant driveway adjacent to Freemont Street. He dropped his bike and stood by the curb. Brock stayed a few feet away. He checked the street for anything suspicious. People raced for good viewing spots of the parade. Crowds stretched three and four feet across sidewalks. Children cheered at dancing clowns. Large balloons floated to the sky. Clowns handed blue, red, green, and yellow balloons to small children. An impatient crowd grew noisier. Young and old waited for the spectacular floats, of all shapes and sizes.

Justin looked up and down the street, as if waiting for someone. He winked. "It's show time, Statler. Ready for your moment of fame?"

He missed something along the way. Brock searched the street again. Two of Justin's friends headed straight for him. He remembered Chad and Robert from school. Chad was a short heavy set guy who sniffed out trouble as he strolled along. Robert was a big machine, bigger than Justin. Long strides controlled a confident walk. Robert approached the ringleader with a jab in the shoulder.

"Hey Zip."

He called Justin by his nickname. They have to be best

friends thought Brock. He wondered why these guys had showed up. Robert and Chad were supposed to be out of town. Brock felt weird having the big guy eye him up and down. He fumbled the change in his pockets. He prayed something would happen so he could leave. The trio gathered in conference making Brock jumpy. Robert and Chad shot looks at him that told him to get out fast. The two new guys weren't sociable about his presence.

"This is your puppet. Stupid Statler! He doesn't know anything. He's one of those special students." Robert laughed hysterically.

Chad joined his buddy. Annoyed by their insults, Brock spoke, "What is a puppet?"

Chad and Robert bent over in agony. They slapped high fives to each other in a fit of laughter.

"Okay guys. Brock asked a question. Which one of us is going to answer him?"

Brock switched glances from Justin to Robert, then Chad to Justin.

"I can't believe you chose stupid Statler this summer," said the big guy.

Brock huddled against his bike, trying to hide when the leader looked back at him. The ringleader chuckled.

"He's perfect for the gang. He doesn't act so stupid either."

The tall guy nudged the ringleader. "Getting friendly with the teacher's dummies. What happened to standards, Zipper? Does that mean we all go down because some kid from special education class decides to take a hike and tattle-tale?"

Justin flinched. He stared at Robert. A brawl brewed and Brock was hypnotized. His body tensed. His stomach muscles knotted. Justin backed off, retreating to the curb.

A bright light clicked on. The Night Hawks existed before

Justin's bright idea. Proof stood on the street before Brock. Coincidence played no part in him joining the gang. He was pre-selected for a special reason. Justin lied about his friends being away and forming a gang that already functioned. Why had the leader lied and then taken his part when teased of being stupid. That was strange coming from someone he didn't know very well.

What kind of gang was he mixed up in? What was a puppet? Questions rattled in the corners of his brain. He kept his distance from the group. Trust was not a personality trait for these guys.

The short boy jumped towards Brock. He stopped inches from him. Warm air exhaled down his neck as a thick arm squeezed his shoulders.

"Look guys, you're scaring the little dumb kid. Are you positive about your puppet decision, Zipper?"

Brock pulled away from the hold. "I don't know what is going on but I'm leaving."

"You going to let your puppet walk away, Zip?" the big guy said.

Brock straddled his bike and pushed off with his foot but he didn't move. Justin held the back tire. He pulled his puppet off the bike, dragging him a couple of meters. "You aren't going anywhere, Statler. We haven't finished what we came to do. Your witnesses would be upset if they gave up holiday time for nothing. We wouldn't want to upset these fellows, now would we?"

Pain ran down Brock's arm. Justin's firm hold pressured his veins. A lump in his throat prevented an answer. Dignity sunk in the pit of his stomach. These guys meant business and all three towered over him. Survival proved slim with any stunts in mind. Cobwebs formed in his head. Ideas scrambled making decisions impossible. He never made wise choices and fright interfered with his thinking.

Justin released his hold. "Come with me."

Cars parked along the street. The leader squatted beside a brown hatchback and dropped his packsack onto the sidewalk. Four-inch spike nails and a small hammer fell from the canvas sack. Brock hugged his chest. Nausea rose and he prayed this wasn't happening. The tall figure hammered a nail into the back tire. Pop! The loud noise cautioned him to suspicious pedestrians.

Marching bands muffled the blowout. No attention focused on the gang. Shock paralyzed Brock.

Justin laughed. "Statler the next vehicle is yours."

The two boys exchanged looks. Brock was immobile. Vandalism was not his game. Two choices seemed apparent: *take consequences for committing a crime and do the time, or stand up to his leader.* This was his cue to show some backbone.

He seized the moment and plunged with all his courage. "I don't destroy other people's property. If that's what the Night Hawks stand for, then I'm out." Brock's stomach twisted. Buttered popcorn filtered the air causing abdominal summersaults. He felt sick to death.

Justin strolled over to Brock, sending a hard stare. "What did you say you were going to do? The oath you took gives me permission to tell you what to do. Is that clear, Statler?"

Brock nodded. He held his stomach tight, fearing its release.

"Just remember the rules and there won't be any trouble. Understand my meaning?"

After another quick nod, Brock realized his actions were deadly. Trouble moved in for the kill as Robert marched towards him. Brock held his breath, squinted his eyes, and waited for broken bones. The big guy passed him, taking a spot near the leader. "Not only is he a dumb puppet but a chicken too. You have your job cut out for you this summer, Zip."

His breakfast shot to his ribcage. Brock had to keep his stomach settled for a little longer. Some adults passed on the road, pausing at the commotion. Two mothers took a good look at the group and continued pushing strollers down the road. One woman turned for a second glance but resumed her pace.

Justin gathered up the long silver spikes and a short wooden handled hammer, shoving them into the blue sack. The packsack flung over his shoulder as he strutted towards his bike. He whispered, "This isn't over, Statler. One week from Friday, you prove that chickens don't exist among the Night Hawks."

The ringleader disappeared with the rest of the gang. Brock trembled. His queasy gut rushed him to the nearest lawn. His stomach gave way, releasing everything inside. Sweaty hands rubbed dirt down the front of his T-shirt. His face was on fire. He dashed away as fast as possible on his beat up bike.

After the experience he encountered Brock grinned knowing he was alive. He thanked his lucky stars for being in one piece. Those guys were quite capable of making mince meat out of him. He took the long way home to sort out the events, which occurred. He considered all facts with care. Brock parked his ten-speed in the yard, thirty minutes later.

Dad repaired an old lawn mower in the basement and the smell of gas seeped upstairs. Brock sneaked down the hall but his dad cornered him at the basement stairs.

"How was the parade this year?"

"Same as usual, Dad."

A ton of bricks hit. Brock lied to his father and it seemed so natural. He rushed to his bedroom for solitude. Music blared with the push of a button. His ghetto blaster drowned out his guilt. He sank into his double bed and shut out the world.

"Brock, are you okay?" His father knocked again. "Brock, do you hear me?"

He opened the door after his father shouted the third time. "Didn't hear you with my music."

"That's a hint to turn the music down. What's the matter, son?"

Brock sat on his bed. "Have you ever heard of a gang having a puppet?"

"A puppet for a mascot?"

"No, someone for their puppet."

His father rested his hands on the desk beside him. "I can't say I recall any such thing. Why are you interested in gangs?"

Brock took a deep breath as his dad's hand slid towards his binder. He jumped from the bed and distracted his father by moving books around on his desk. "I was just wondering."

"What's this?" Dad pointed to the closed binder on the desk.

"I thought I'd take out a binder with loose leaf paper in case I decided to practice my writing."

"Great stuff! That's a good way to improve your reading and writing skills."

"I didn't think it would hurt to practice once in awhile over the holidays before getting my new computer."

"Impressive or what. I'm heading back to fix that old clunker for Mr. Wilson's neighbor. See you later."

Everything seemed complicated. Brock lied to his father the second time. A puzzle danced in his head. None of the pieces connected. The facts pointed to one important issue. Justin tricked him from the beginning. The Night Hawks showed up at the parade expecting to be there for Brock's initiation. It seemed he was chosen as a puppet for the summer. Each summer Justin picked a different person.

Questions popped into Brock's head intensifying interest. He wanted excitement, adventure, and now he had found it. His challenge to change himself seemed simple at first. Everything exploded into a full-fledged mystery.

He glanced at his grandfather's picture on the night table. *"You are the only one who can help me decide what to do."* His grandpa's smile enveloped him into serene thought.

"Grandpa, I have so many unanswered questions and everything seems complicated. I have to find out what the Night Hawks represent and why I am chosen as a puppet. I don't even know what a puppet does."

Brock ran his fingertips over the smooth color photograph. He closed his eyes.

"Why did Justin make a big issue about joining a gang that already existed? Was popping tires a regular act of Justin's or was it part of his initiation?"

Brock wondered if Justin had a criminal record. Nothing was mentioned around school but the scar was unusual for a thirteen-year-old boy.

He placed the picture back in its spot. Brock had one big problem. *"Grandpa, I don't know all the details of being a member with the Night Hawks. I do want to belong to a group and hang out with my classmates but this initiation is scary. After seeing Justin vandalize private property I don't know what kind of prank he expects of me. I don't know if I should participate. I took an oath and it frightens me when I think what might happen if I disobey the rules."*

Brock considered his options. Maybe Justin asked for his choice of prank to prove his loyalty to the gang. He thought if he showed his ability, he would gain acceptance as a full pledged gang member. This test proved he wasn't a chicken.

That's it! Brock figured a practical joke never hurt anyone and it promised him high ranking with his ringleader. His next plan of action showed his risk-taking side. Once again he had to take a stance. Kids pulled pranks every day, what was complicated about a harmless stunt?

3

STRINGS ARE ACTIVATED

Brock arrived at his new job Tuesday morning. Dad gave him a quick tour of Wilson's Auto Garage. He visited the shop many times but this morning felt like his first. Brock waited at the door excited for his instructions. Oil and grease increased eagerness to begin work. His hands itched for the slippery solution. Dad's three-tier tool chest sat in the far corner. Shelves hung behind his father's metal chest. Wooden shelving weighed down with tools, parts, containers, and different sized packages. A large hoist supported a jeep in mid air. The hoist hovered above the vehicle while two men worked on it.

Brock consumed all the activity. His last visit to Wilson's Garage seemed years ago. The phone interrupted his thoughts. Dad answered the wall phone in the shop.

Reality sunk in at eight o'clock. Brock stood next to his dad, listening to instructions. A mechanic's job interested him and meant learning everything.

"I'm starting you off stacking the old tires laying around outside in the back. Stack them at the side of the garage as high as you can reach. When you're done we have work on that pickup truck over there."

Brock nodded. His body jumped with anticipation. Compared to enthusiastic limbs his mind slithered. The morning seemed like a fantasy come true. The pickup truck inspired him to begin on the tires. Working on a vehicle was the last job he ever imagined.

He headed outside for his first duty. Brock checked the dirty old tires scattered around the yard. After lifting one tire, he decided rolling it was quicker. He raced against the heat beaming down.

The sun's rays sparkled on the pavement, reflecting on metal rims stacked against the building. Shining rims impaired vision, making Brock concentrate on the tires. He hurried before he couldn't handle the heated rubber. After an hour of piling used tires he was anxious to check out the old truck waiting for repairs in the shop.

Three piles of black rubber sat against the wall. Brock admired his completed chore. A dampened T-shirt covered in black stuck to his chest. He rubbed sweat and dirt from his forehead with a swipe of his arm. The hard work was over, he thought. The easy stuff waited inside.

He wasn't old enough for full-time work with the company, but Mr. Wilson offered him odd jobs around the shop for the summer. Student wages were better than no pay. Brock picked up garbage, scrap metal, tools, and ran from one mechanic to the other with parts. His status made him proud.

The first week of work inspired Brock. He spent extra time with his father and watched every move around the shop. His second week zoomed by even faster. The shop sparkled. A big surprise came Thursday afternoon. Brock grabbed a soft drink from his metal lunch pail and sat on an empty container. Fifteen-minutes flew by enjoying time with his co-workers. All morning Dad was in a super mood. Brock sipped the refreshing drink savoring each mouthful.

Dad approached him with a steaming cup of coffee in his hand. "Well son, your second week of work is almost finished. How is the job going?"

The other employees sat in a group. Brock felt like one of them. He shifted in his seat when the other men looked at him. "It's great." It was weird having Dad speak to him like an employee. He aged ten years and matured from the adult conversations concerning work.

"That's good. You have done a terrific job and the men are impressed." Dad pointed to the group of men. "The guys suggested Mr. Wilson keep you on for weekends when school starts."

Brock was shocked. "Really?" Three men sitting on plastic crates confirmed the news by clapping.

Brock tilted his head hiding a burning face. "A weekend job sounds fantastic. I'll be able to earn money all year."

Dad's hand touched his shoulder. A big smile crossed his father's face. "This must be your lucky day, son."

"What do you mean, Dad?" Brock shifted closer for more news.

"Remember the customers who bought your grandfather's birdhouses. Well, calls have come in and some people are interested in buying more houses. They asked if you would consider following in your grandfather's footsteps."

Brock gasped. "They want me to build them. I haven't worked on one since springtime."

Dad squeezed his shoulders and winked, "Something to think about. Nothing would please your grandfather more than having you take over his business."

"I could do it for Grandpa." Brock lowered his head in

remembrance.

"It would be your own business. This is a decision to make because you want to do it, not because you feel obligated. Grandpa would understand either way. If there is anything I can do to help, just ask."

Adrenaline pumped through Brock's veins. He leaped for his dad, knocking over the container. He wrapped his arms around his father's neck. "Thanks Dad. I'd be proud to take over Grandpa's work. I'll need wood, nails, paint…"

"Okay, I get the picture. Make a list and we'll pick up what you need on the weekend. Coffee break is over men. Back to work."

Brock resumed his cleaning duties and a quick lesson on oil changes. Five o'clock came and he locked up shop with his dad. He completed his day turning off all the lights and double checking all machines.

A burst of energy recharged Brock. "What do I do first Dad? I know I have to make a list of supplies, and I already have an idea what is in the shed. Where will I work? When will I call the people and tell them I've started building bird…"

"Whoa, son! Take it one step at a time."

"There is so much to do and I don't know what to do first?" Brock was hyper and couldn't sit still.

"Son, make a list of supplies and we'll pick them up on the weekend. I'll give you the customer names to contact. Take their orders and give them an idea when they can expect delivery."

"Sounds easy when you say it."

Dad laughed. "It is easy. The hard part is the carpenter work."

"I have to figure out what hours I can work and how much to charge. Where will I build?"

"What's wrong with your grandfather's workshop?"

Brock sprung from his seat remembering the strapped seatbelt. "Ouch!" He rubbed his stomach. "I can use the workshop downstairs. I thought that was your room since Grandpa's gone."

"No son, it's our room. It might take you some time to clean up in there. I'll give you a hand since most of the mess is mine from working on lawnmowers and rotor tillers. Summer brings all kinds of repairs for people maintaining gardens."

"This is so neat. I never imagined owning my own business." Ideas circulated, forming new and improved birdhouses. "I will earn my own money, control sales and profits. I can make as much as I want and it is all mine."

"You're talking like a true business person but don't get carried away. You will have to sell a few houses to pay for supplies. There might not be a profit for a little bit."

"I guess there is a lot of work before I get paid." Brock sighed. "Looks like my holidays are getting busy."

Brock remembered time spent with his grandfather. Building birdhouses past the time in a calm manner. He enjoyed learning about the old days. Stories about his family history remained in Brock's heart. The kind of knowledge that only a grandparent offered. A sharp pain jabbed his chest. He missed the good times with his grandfather.

It seemed funny, only a couple of days ago Brock spotted a birdhouse in the shed and now he operated the business. What drew him closer to his grandfather, coincidence or loneliness?

Dad had detoured for a large pizza with the works. Inside the house, Dad dropped the hot cardboard box onto the counter. "Let's celebrate Brock. Grab a plate and dig in. This has been an exciting day for you hasn't it?"

"Sure has. I can't wait to tell Trenton. He won't believe what has happened the past few weeks." Justin came to mind the second the words slipped off his tongue. He had more to tell his friend than his father ever imagined. "Maybe I can offer him partners in the birdhouse business and we can both run it." Dad laughed. "Sounds like you boys are going to have quite a reunion."

Brock chewed his pizza. He shoved stringy mozzarella cheese, pepperoni, and mushrooms into his mouth without a breath. Cooked onions hid under his napkin as usual. If events continued at this rate Brock faced more challenges than expected.

"Slow down there. The pizza won't run away."

Brock swallowed his last bite. Under his breath he jabbered, "I have so much to do I better start right away. Tomorrow is Friday and I need a list of supplies ready so we can pick them up at the hardware store Saturday."

Dad smiled.

Dinner ended with a large slice of chocolate cake Dad had hidden in the fridge. A tall frosted glass of milk washed down the perfect meal. Energy rushed through Brock's body. He sprung for the basement when Dad called, "Brock can you clean up in here. I want to start the laundry."

"No problem." Brock scurried about the kitchen. He washed the dishes and set them in the rack to drip-dry. He wiped off the counter and table and ran for the doorway. He spun on his heels. He rushed the leftover pizza into the fridge, box and all. The kitchen was spotless. A thumb up in the air permitted an exit.

The doorbell halted his second attempt for the basement. Brock ran down the hallway to the entrance sliding across the linoleum floor. One hand opened the front door as his other hand covered his mouth.

Justin Galley stood with his hand braced against the

doorframe. A blank stare greeted Brock. Beads of sweat covered the leaders red face. He raised a fist. A hard thump beat against his left hand.

Brock jumped backwards. Panic and fear pounded heavy in his chest.

"Need to talk. Come on."

"I'm busy doing chores. Can't this wait?"

Justin stepped inside the entrance grabbing Brock by the front of his T-shirt, "You are coming with me now. We have trouble."

Brock nodded. Justin let go and Brock raced to the basement stairs. His calm voice cracked before he finished speaking. "I'm going out Dad. See you in a bit."

Brock followed his ringleader outside. They stopped at the end of the driveway. Justin plunked down onto the curb. Two minutes later, he stood. He paced in a circle without speaking.

Brock never moved. Dizziness crept over him watching his leader go round and round. From a safe distance, he observed Justin raise and lower his hands beside his body. His fists clenched to punch someone or something. Brock sensed something terrible had occurred because Justin was so angry. Every minute waiting for an explanation increased his heart rate. A cold glass of water sounded good at that moment. His body temperature shot upward until the tall figure stopped moving.

"Cops came to my place last night," Justin blurted.

"What happened?"

The ringleader circled the ground again. His hands kept fidgeting. Red fists turned white.

"They warned me to leave old man Challens alone or I would be charged. I cut through his place going to school and he warned me to stay off his property. He put up a 'No

Trespassing' sign, but that didn't stop me. He told me next time he was calling the cops. I trashed his place to stop him from threatening me."

Brock listened to an unbelievable story. He wondered why Justin was telling him all this stuff. "Mr. Challens called the police!"

"Guess so, but that's no big deal. I have ways to fix the old man. My stepfather is the problem. He went nuts after the cops left. My old man yelled at me for an hour. He went crazy because I pestered a senior citizen."

Justin's right eye looked dark and he kept turning his head away. Brock decided to find out more. "Did your dad hit you?"

The ringleader looked down at Brock exposing his face. A black and purple goose egg stuck out from Justin's eye.

Mr. Galley running out of the house with a baseball bat in his hand stuck in Brock's mind. The terrified look on Justin's face rushed to the surface of his thoughts. "Is this because the police showed up at your house?"

Justin chuckled. "What was the first clue?" He switched to a serious tone. "I don't have to do anything to be used as a punching bag. My old man thinks he has a hard day working with numbers and having his clients get on his nerves so he gets drunk when he comes home. After he's wasted it is declared pick on Justin time. Why do you think I go out every night?"

It never crossed Brock's mind. He shrugged off the pain his heart endured at that moment. His friend's shiner kicked in a sympathetic ear.

"My mom is a nurse on afternoon shift. My dad, or stepfather, comes home around five-thirty. That's when I leave. Once he starts boozing that's my clue to run."

That's why Justin spent so much time on the street at night, thought Brock.

"What happens when you go home afterwards, Justin? Does your father get upset because you've been gone so long?"

"The old guy is passed out and the house is quiet by then. I get so mad at him and I have to go out. I take it out on other people but nobody gets hurt. A few pranks here and there and it's time to go home."

Brock felt sorry for his ringleader's family life. He disapproved of Justin's pranks but wasn't about to confront him. This guy's rage terrified Brock when released. Justin's moods confused him. He changed from a happy-go-lucky guy to a hunted animal out for revenge within minutes. Brock addressed him with careful words because anything could tick off the leader. His new friend was a time bomb set to explode.

A crafted person such as Justin had to have good qualities. Brock knew his leader must have a good side no matter how destructive he presented himself.

A great day at work put Brock in a generous frame of mind. His leader settled down and took control. He shared his sympathy trying to help a troubled friend. "I wish I could do something, Justin." At that moment, Brock swallowed his foot. Considering the lump in his throat, his ankle too.

The day passed without any worries about his initiation until now. He had just introduced the subject.

"Actually Statler, your time has come to show you are a true Night Hawk. It's time to prove nobody tells me what to do. It's payback for Challens and he'll wish he never knew Justin Galley."

Brock foreseen a terrible event and interrupted, "What does that have to do with me and why did you say earlier that 'we' were in trouble?"

Justin leaned over resting his arm on Brock's shoulder. The leader tapped his head and whispered, "You are my puppet. I pull the strings and you dance. Have you forgotten our code puppet boy? One gets in trouble we all take the heat."

The creepy voice spooked Brock. Justin acted like an insane character out of a horror picture. A quick jerk released him from the stranger. He stepped aside remaining speechless. A glance towards the living room window told him he was on his own.

"Nothing to be scared about Statler. We do the job and it's over. Simple as one, two, three. You do know how to count! This will be your initiation. Be at the corner of Dalewood and Martin on Saturday night. Fun begins at seven-thirty sharp."

Justin pulled away on his bike. Brock waved, "Wait! Hold on a minute." The ringleader was gone in a flash.

Brock released a heavy sigh. This was serious. Justin wasn't the one in trouble, he was. The ringleader cornered him into a crime of revenge on an old man whom he had never met.

A puppet acted out the commands of its leader. Brock wished the Night Hawks found another puppet for their activities. Upcoming weekend events horrified him.

Brock slipped inside sneaking downstairs to the workshop. The blaring television blocked out any noise he made.

Brock searched the small room for his grandfather's wood supplies. Wooden shelves lined the walls. Dad collected woodworking tools and utensils over the years. He always kept the basics Grandpa needed for his pieces of art.

An old birdhouse rested against a paint can. One side needed repairs. Brock swelled with inspiration. He held the tiny house in the palms of his hands. He sniffed the wood, generating special moments from the past. Rough edges outlined the roof. He traveled his index finger along the design. A sliver jabbed into his finger making him jolt. The birdhouse was Grandpa's last project. The house in the shed was the last one both of them worked on as a team.

His grandfather's presence filled the room with joy. Brock escaped his fears if only for the time being. He spotted the hand sander sitting on a shelf in front of him. One repair after another passed into two hours of work.

Brock nailed the broken side of the birdhouse. He sanded and prepared it for painting. The small house had one perch and open in the front. The roof extended far enough for protection from the rain. A simple version created by Grandpa when Brock first learned the basics of woodworking.

Pleased by his progress in a short period, Brock set the bird's home back onto the shelf. He cleaned his mess and went to bed.

The night dragged on. Brock tossed and turned in bed. Thoughts of his new business mixed with flashes of Justin. His ringleader threatened his participation in an act of revenge. He knew what the oath meant but getting out of the Night Hawks was a realistic solution.

He wondered what kind of holiday Trenton was having. He waited for his buddy's call but never received one. Trenton was lucky. He had a variety of chores on the farm to occupy his time. A fall fair scheduled for the first week in August sounded like fun. Brock never attended a fall fair like they had in small rural areas. Northshore had flea markets where area farmers sold baking, preserves, and fresh fruits and vegetables. The flea markets never had horses, cows, sheep, pigs, chickens and hens to see.

It was late. Brock received his first paycheck the next day and was excited. He focused on work and figured how much money he would deposit into his savings account. He listed items he wanted to purchase with his earnings.

Number one priority was paying his dad's way to the Northshore Summer Festival. He was determined to treat his dad for the whole night out. He surprised his father with little gifts and this was something special. The Summer Festival was the largest event during the summer and the Statler family attended every year.

The Night Hawks episode and Justin Galley exhausted Brock. He had one day left before his initiation. His mind went blank as time ran out before Friday. This weekend required all the brainpower he could master since his initiation was handed to him on a silver platter. An emergency plan seemed urgent in case his initiation backfired. Brock sunk deeper to prove himself as the weeks transformed. He became desperate to fight his way out of this mess alone and prove he could take the heat like Justin's gang. Which 'heat' would it be?

4

ON THE RUN

Friday was payday! Brock's proficient work produced a well-organized shop. Dad explained steps in changing tires and performing a tune-up on a small Cavalier car. Each day increased his mechanical knowledge and heightened work opportunities.

The eight-hour shift zoomed by. Dad handed Brock his first paycheck at five o'clock.

"Don't spend it all in one place, son."

"I already have plans for my money. Speaking of plans, is it okay if I head to the mall after dinner?" Brock squeezed the white envelope. The crisp paper felt like gold between his fingers. Excitement squirmed for freedom through knotted muscles.

Dad rubbed his head and he felt his short hairs tangle. "Sure. Don't be out too late tonight."

Brock rushed around the kitchen preparing dinner with his dad. He was wound tighter than a yo-yo ready for a play of walk the dog. Food wasted time with no appetite to nourish. He picked at his meal for a few minutes. "May I be excused?"

Dad smiled. "Go ahead and deposit that cheque."

"Thanks Dad." Brock bounced off his seat and out the door in a flash.

The bank was busy at Northshore Mall. Experience reminded Brock that Friday night was the worst time for banking. People lined up from the bank entrance waiting their turn. Four tellers prepared bankbooks and punched in numbers on computers. The line took forever crawling forward to the next available teller. Overwhelmed by the wait Brock became light-headed. The air conditioning can't be working he thought as his pay envelope stuck to his hand.

A short woman in her late fifties welcomed Brock with a wide smile. "What can I do for you today, sir?"

Filled with pride he handed over his big pay. "I would like to deposit one-hundred and seventy dollars. This is my bank book." Brock cooled down and relaxed.

"You must have worked hard for this much money." The teller smiled.

Brock shifted behind the counter. "I'd like to keep some money too."

"We'll fix you right up here, sir."

The woman finalized Brock's transaction. He received his spending money and left the bank. He walked high above the clouds. His cheerful state was unbreakable.

Brock had no time to spend money since he started work. He became stingy saving every penny. He owed it all to the bèst teacher for showing him the importance of saving money. Every year Dad purchased a special item for the house. This year a new computer waited to occupy his small desk.

Computer class was required for grade seven and eight classes. Practice became an essential part of learning the computer programs used in Junior High School. That meant improved reading and writing skills so he could learn independently at home.

Brock took the long route through the mall. He checked out items on sale in store windows. Teenagers rushed here and there. People shoved through the main corridor.

A cold drink sounded like an excellent idea until Brock reached the food fair. The place was packed and no available seats. Customers waited for service at the submarine place, Chinese contender, hamburger joint, and pizza place. Dinnertime turned the food court into rush hour for take-out or eat-in meals.

Brock passed through the food section to the back mall entrance. He had locked his ten-speed in the bike rack outside the main doors. A graceful stride floated him outside. Satisfied with his achievements for the day and having money in his pocket he unlocked his bike.

Snap, snap! Brock turned around. Someone was bent over a small red bike. The two-wheeler was no bigger than twenty-four inches. The bike connected to a mesh fence that divided the mall property from homes on the other side. *Snap, snap!* The person straightened up and turned his way.

Justin Galley held a pair of bolt cutters in his hands. The fourteen-inch long cutters included a pair of wide teeth on the end. Justin squeezed the rubber handles together around the linked bike lock. Bolt cutters made the job easy. A final snip cut through the chain. The green plastic covering dropped to the ground.

Brock jerked to free his bike from the rack. Danger followed trouble and he wasn't getting caught in a theft scene. Too late! The mall doors swung open and a big man dressed in a gray uniform walked out. Brock stood a meter away from the tall security guard carrying a radio in his hand.

The guard spotted Justin. Authority traveled from deep inside, "Hey! What do you think you're doing?"

Justin yanked the bike free from the mesh fence. He hopped onto the small frame holding the long cutters in his hand. Sailing past Brock, he shouted, "Let's get out of here."

Dazed and confused, Brock turned to face a stern looking man. The security guard raised the radio to his mouth. Static played from the guard's hand. The bike jammed between the bars. Brock jiggled the frame sideways releasing it from the rack. The man sprung forward. Brock hit the seat full force making a getaway.

By the skin of his teeth, he passed parked cars in the narrow lane. He bolted out of control, avoiding a collision from his reckless steering. Brock bounced full speed onto Copper Street.

Justin pedaled in high gear ahead but Brock gained on him. The road came to a bend and his leader continued straight for Mackey Avenue. He never looked back. Brock stayed close on his leader's tail. He knew he would crash into a parked car if he checked behind.

The ringleader turned left onto Mackey Avenue. A dead end street branched off at the next corner. Justin followed the dead end. He passed a church in progress. Cars parked down each side of the gravel road. Brock rode like a maniac down the middle of the road. He avoided scraping vehicles along his route.

The road opened into a turn around where a large hydro substation situated on the left. A tall metal fence ran around the high voltage area. Transformers generated high volume of power and were clearly posted as dangerous. Justin picked a serious place to hide.

Brock pulled alongside the stolen bike. "What in the world do you think you are doing? That security guard had a good look at me and you involved me as your partner in crime. I can't believe you called me to hurry up."

"You were watching me so I guess that makes you an accomplice. What's the big deal? You escaped didn't you, and wasn't it a rush pumping blood through your veins like that?"

Brock shook his head. He slammed his palms down on the handles. He refused the pain shooting through his wrists.

"We have a temper do we."

Brock studied the area surrounding them. Trees fenced off the clearing leading to paths in all directions into the bush. He watched down the road past the church.

"You did it this time, Justin. Now I am involved in a theft I never committed and I am stuck with you until it is safe to leave here. Why do you stir up trouble and include me all the time?"

"You were the one looking for excitement this summer. I provide it for you and now you chicken out as usual. Statler, you're a hard one to please."

Brock's urge to knock sense into his leader diminished because size difference scared him. Fleeing the site was an option if he wanted handcuffed by the police. He was stuck hiding out with a thief.

Justin dropped the small bike and walked away laughing. He inched closer to the substation. Crime was one thing but fooling around with an electrical power supply was crazy.

"Get away from there. You aren't playing with a toy. You want to get fried?"

Justin stopped. He stared at Brock as he inched closer. "Have we taken smart pills today, Statler? Maybe I want some excitement while we wait. How many objects do you think I can sizzle?"

Brock stalled the leader. "You want to get electrocuted. Didn't you read in the paper about that kid who died? Some kids were playing around one of these substations just like you are now and one of them never made it home. Maybe that's exactly what you hope will happen." Justin paused at the fence. Weight dropped when Brock thought he got through to the leader.

"Statler, you're such a wimp. I'm not hoping for anything. Come join the fun, or if you're so tough come and stop me. I'd have the job done and out of here before you make a move."

The whole situation disgusted Brock. A conversation carried on with a corpse received better results. He decided distance from this guy and the substation was smart until he could leave. Brock played enough mind games with the leader. He turned his bike to leave the scene when two men headed in his direction. He dropped the bike, running for the nearest bush.

Brock waved at Justin to get out of sight. The two men approached the clearing. The men dressed in two-piece dark suits like undercover cops. Panic struck as the men stopped a few meters away. Voices mumbled in conversation. Brock remained breathless for fear the men would hear him breathing. Unexpected air released from his lungs and he choked. A quick reflex shot his hand over his mouth. He inhaled short and fast through his nose. He felt a sneeze building and counted to ten.

The men turned back towards the parked cars. Brock removed his hand to release a deep sigh. Branches rustled close by. He grabbed his chest taking a deep breath. A rapid search through the bush relieved suspicion of movement. A large frame fell out of the shrubs on his right side.

"You trying to give me a heart attack. Don't pull that stunt on me again." Brock fell backwards onto dried leaves and twigs. He resumed normal breathing for a minute as he lay silent.

Justin grabbed his sides in a fit of laughter.

"You think that was a big joke. Those guys could have been police officers."

"Whatever, Statler. I found a spot to hide out for a while. Come on, it's not too far from here."

Brock sneaked across the clearing hunched over like a convict. The bush opened up on the other side of the hydro substation. Flat rock formed a hill about four meters high. The open space elevated to the top of the rock.

Brock crawled up the slope reaching a smooth gray platform. Large evergreen boughs surrounded them. Branches provided a lookout for any unusual activity. The church positioned right across the road. Mackey Avenue sat in perfect view off to the right. Sheltered in a cozy haven where nobody could see him, Brock felt safe.

A long body stretched out beside him. The ringleader acted like he was tanning on the beaches in Bermuda.

"None of this bothers you in the least, does it? It's all one never ending adventure."

Justin opened his packsack. Out came a crate of eggs, which he placed between his slender legs. A long arm extended, offering Brock an egg. "Want to pass some time while we wait for the cops to turn up a cold trail."

"You're crazy. The police have been called by now and looking for us this minute. Here you are ready for the next stage of trouble. What is the matter with you?"

"Once a chicken, always a chicken." Justin stood and flapped his arms. "Cluck, cluck, cluck." He snickered and practiced his pitching shots. Eggs barreled across the road. "One little chicky, two little chickies, three little chickies." Eggs splattered against car windshields, flying one after another.

Brock covered his head. Sounds increased with each

splattering egg. He was paranoid people from the church heard the noise. Justin's anger intensified with each throw. The eggs hit harder and harder until they were all gone.

Brock checked the church grounds but no one moved on the property. "That is the lowest thing I have ever seen anyone perform. How do you sleep at night, Justin Galley? You destroy personal property, not to mention outside of a church and why? What have those people done to you?" Brock figured the usual reply was coming and he shook his head in disgust.

A swift hand grabbed his throat. Gasps of air forced through his lungs. Pain shot down his neck and into his throat. Brock tore at the hands wrapped around his windpipe but couldn't remove them. He coughed and choked fighting for air.

The large hands let go. Justin's devil eyes transfixed Brock. Evil spirits connected consuming all of his energy.

A calm, rational voice escaped from the leader. "It only takes one person to make you mad. One person caused more trouble for me than a whole town of people. Revenge is my motto."

"You really need help, Justin. No one has that much hatred. Who made you so mad?"

The leader shrugged. "Maybe I enjoy being mean. It is spontaneous fun. It sure beats cleaning your room, taking out garbage, doing dishes, and all those female jobs."

Brock attacked, "Wait one minute. I don't have a mother, so who do you think cleans, cooks, and does laundry at my place? You have both parents and you complain about little things. What about some of your friends who come from broken homes? What kinds of lives do they live? You don't see them causing trouble when they don't get their way."

Justin leaned in for the kill. Brock jumped out of reach sliding down the slope. He landed flat on his back. Heavy weight pounded down on him. Brock smothered underneath. Trapped arms and legs crushed by the bully on top of him. Justin pressed all one hundred and twenty-three pounds of dead weight on Brock's stomach and chest. Held to the ground like contact cement his hands inched out from under the heavy legs. One hand swung at the assailant's chest. The second arm freed itself striking the strangers face.

Justin lost his balance. Brock surprised himself with an unexpected reaction. The leader fell to the side and Brock crawled out. Panic struck like falling bricks. He staggered to his bike. Renewed strength ran through his limbs. An ounce of energy nourished his legs saving his life as he motored past the clearing. A tall figure leaped from the bush hitting the back tire. Enveloped by terror Brock controlled his swerving bike with precision.

Unharmed, Brock encountered the fastest ride in history. He returned home with shirt on his back and emotions shaken. He slipped through the back door letting his father know he was home.

He sneaked down to the basement. Brock spent time alone getting his act together. His nerves shot from another bone chilling escape. He sat on the wooden stool in the corner of the room settling a knotted stomach. He hugged his knees tight and lowered his head. His eyes filled, releasing a flow of tears.

Brock confronted his ringleader head on and regretted it. He made the mistake of a lifetime. He knew a severe punishment followed his actions. Anger and frustration reached a boiling point. He blew a fuse and spoke out. Brock wasn't sure about his new image. He had excitement and all the adventure he asked for but circumstances pointed towards legal action.

Minutes dragged into an hour. Brock's father called. He wiped his face and cleared his throat. "Coming Dad."

Dad met him at the top of the stairs. "Busy at the woodworking are you. I'm calling it an early night son. Don't stay up too late and I'll see you in the morning."

Brock checked the doors and stretched out on the sofa. He curled up with his mother's homemade quilt, soaking in memories. Aching muscles relaxed. Confusion prevented him from concentrating on television. His attention switched to problems with Justin. An hour later Brock went to bed. Horror drained all emotions. Fatigue smothered his aching body and reality disappeared into his dreams.

Saturday morning supplied a chain of interesting events. Dad drank his coffee and read the morning paper. Dad concentrated on the front page for some time. Brock noticed a definite interest because his father usually skimmed through the pages from front to back. He picked the most interesting sections to read. Lakeside Daily offered a small publication with little news. Exciting events were rare in Northshore.

Brock poured himself a large glass of orange juice distracting his suspicions. "Aren't we a dedicated reader this morning?" Brock seated himself opposite his dad at the table.

His father lifted his head. "Juvenile crime is on the rise again. Just when you think they have caught all those youngsters another one pops his head."

Startled by his father's reaction Brock inquired about details. "Where is this Dad?" He knew first hand, that crime rose in his neighborhood.

"I'm almost finished and you can read it for yourself. You should be reading more on the weekends anyway."

Aggravated by the wait, Brock grabbed a slice of cold pizza from the fridge. A couple of bites later he sat down with the newspaper.

"That isn't a healthy breakfast for a boy your age. Want

some bacon and eggs?"

"Pizza is fine Dad. It will hold me over until lunch." Brock picked up the paper and began reading. In large capital letters he sounded out the words:

"*VAN-DAL-ISM*
ON THE RISE
IN WEST END
NEIGH-BOR-HOOD"

Suspense killed him as he continued reading. It was difficult pronouncing some words and he couldn't read fast enough to get to the good part. Brock took his best shot. He read what he could grasp in the general idea by the end of the article.

"Oh, no!"

Mr. Statler dropped what he was reading. "What's the matter Brock?"

Both barrels aimed straight at Brock's head. The article gave a vague description of Justin and him as the offenders. Theft at the mall was reported and the guard described the juveniles involved. A criminal record advanced a step closer to reality.

"Nothing," Brock quivered, realizing he spoke aloud.

Police investigations began into all recent crimes reported. The victims all lived in his neighborhood. The article stated that a couple of youths were suspects. That meant police would be questioning them soon.

Brock raced for the washroom and locked the door. It seemed liked ages passed. His breakfast disagreed with him. A glance in the mirror confirmed Brock was face to face with a ghost.

Dad knocked at the door. "Time to leave for work son."

Brock offered extra hours at the shop that day because it was Saturday. New developments changed his plans. A sick day appeared out of thin air. "I don't feel too good. I think you were right about the pizza Dad. My stomach feels sick."

His father waited a minute. "Sure you don't want me to stay home? I don't have any emergencies."

Brock sheltered his fear. He hated lying to his father but it had become a common practice. "I'll be fine. See you at dinner." He wasn't fine and nothing would solve this problem any time soon. He headed for juvenile court if he didn't find a solution as soon as possible.

The Statler families ranked high as law-abiding citizens and were never charged of any crime. The law remained on their side. They minded their own business and expected others to do the same. Brock became the black sheep of the family within weeks. A criminal record called his name shaming his grandfather's family.

Brock searched the telephone directory. He called Justin's phone number but a machine answered. He repeated the call and no luck. He rode to the leader's house to pay a personal visit and no one answered the door.

Time ran out and desperate measures took precedence. Brock suspected more going on than what his leader led him to believe. Justin's run in with the police stemmed from a long time ago and Brock thought his support might help his leader.

He rode around the neighborhood and no sign of his new friend. He took a spin downtown, around the parks, the pool halls, arcades, and the mall. Justin was nowhere. It dawned on him that maybe his ringleader read the morning paper. Maybe he was hiding from the police.

Brock returned home. He concentrated on an appropriate course of action in the matter but nothing came to mind. Serious thinking came easier in his workshop so he hid out for a few hours.

He worried over his new friend. He wasn't sure why he

cared about this guy. Justin made him an accomplice twice. Brock's compassion brought out his humane side leaving him with guilt if he didn't try to get help for Justin. His friend seemed helpless and yet forceful. Brock approached his next level of challenges. Investigator was the last straw. He decided relaxing to take his mind off pressures. A new birdhouse called his name.

Safety surrounded Brock as usual. His grandfather watched over him at all times. Tension released filling him with hope for achievement. He felt a renewed strength overcome his weary bones.

Hours passed and a new creation was born. Brock pleased himself with a beautiful birdhouse.

"Looks like your woodworking will survive after all, Grandpa. I wish I could say the same for Justin. Why won't he stay out of trouble and concentrate on his creative abilities? He has great potential in building go-carts. Why am I so concerned about what happens to Justin? He's caused nothing but chaos in my life since we started hanging out. The Night Hawks have been the worst thing I could have joined and I can't get out of it."

Brock sniffed sprouting tears. *"Grandpa, I learned a lesson of life the hard way. If you were here, I wouldn't have made a terrible mistake. I only wanted to fill the emptiness of being alone. You and Mom left and now Trenton. I took the job at Wilson's Garage so I could spend more time with Dad. That didn't fill the gap. I guess challenging myself was a huge mistake and now I'm involved with the law. Give me some idea how to make this mess go away."*

Brock prayed for guidance from his grandfather. He had a difficult choice to make. He would either help Justin as a friend and give him support with his abuse, or he would quit the Night

Hawks taking the punishment and let his leader deal with his own problems. The last option appeared painful. What was Brock's decision?

5

ZIPPER'S CREATIVE RAGE

A week passed and no sign of Justin. It wasn't like him not showing up unannounced and complaining about family issues. Brock sensed trouble and it bothered him. Justin confided in him for a reason. It was obvious that the guy had nobody to talk to. Brock feared his leader had been beaten once again, maybe serious this time.

The diminished visits welcomed less tension for Brock and at the same time, intuition warned that something bad had happened. An unsettled feeling aggravated a nervous reaction.

Wilson's Auto Garage supplied steady work and payday as motivation. Brock grew independent and his job boosted self-confidence. Unlike other boys his age, weekly allowances were unavailable.

On Friday night, Brock returned to his workshop as planned. He tidied up the scattered wood scraps on his table.

Dad surprised him with a visit. "The carpenter is hard at it. Sales must be climbing."

"I finished three birdhouses and signed on two more customers last week."

63

Dad examined a freshly painted house. A swallow's house caught his attention. A smile appeared. "Your grandfather would be proud, son. This is quality work."

Management skills proved satisfying in Brock's new business. "I've increased production by scheduling regular hours during weeknights. The toughest part is keeping track of expenses."

Dad laughed, patting Brock on the back. "Doesn't seem to be any waste of supplies. At this rate you'll be able to buy that new computer all by yourself."

Brock stuck out his lower lip and pouted. "Business isn't that great, but I'm getting the orders out on record time." He motioned around the room. "It is a little messy right now. Work does come before housecleaning."

Dad departed with a final word. "Almost forgot why I came down. Justin is upstairs."

Brock fumbled the piece of roofing in his hands. He noticed a curious look from his dad. He wondered what had happened to his leader but enjoyed time working on his hobbies. Justin's appearance brought back sudden nervousness. Brock put the roof on the workbench and followed his dad.

The ringleader waited inside the entrance. He shifted weight from one foot to the other. He shoved his hands inside ripped pockets.

Brock paused. Slow and steady, he approached his visitor. The leader folded his hands over his chest.

"Time for a meeting," ordered the ringleader.

Brock looked over his shoulder. He clasped his hands in a whisper, "Have you read the paper?"

"What are you talking about?"

Brock led the tall boy outside. He found a private place and lowered his voice, "Didn't you read the newspaper last week?

Police are looking for two offenders. The mall security guard gave a perfect description of you."

Justin flew his hands above his head. "So what? They never caught anyone. We have more trouble than some newspaper article."

"What could be more important than having the police after you?"

The ringleader cracked his knuckles making horrible sounds. "Listen here Statler. The puppet's work is not finished. You have to help me prove to my step-father how creative I am."

Brock held up his hands. "I'm not getting involved in any more of your schemes. Here I've been worried sick about you while you've been working on another wild scheme."

Justin gave his puppet a funny look. He snapped back to present and explained, "My old man figures I have no purpose in life. Hanging around all summer without a job is wasted time. I should spend time being more creative." Justin waved his arms in anger.

"Sounds like your problem, not mine. Did you ever think maybe your father has a point?"

Justin shoved his finger into Brock's face. "You have more guts than you did a few weeks ago. Either you are a dummy, Statler, or you're getting a little too brave." The leader rested his hands on his hips. "Tonight Justin Galley proves how creative he is. Your job is being guard and making sure I have all the supplies I need. You might get some action of your own." The leader tossed the packsack to Brock.

The bag felt heavy. Brock looked at the front door.

"Don't even think about it. You are in this as deep as I am. Remember, as a Night Hawk member you take orders from me." Justin hopped on his bike and looked back at Brock. "By the way puppet, you don't want to know what I do to chickens. The police would love to nail their suspect." Justin rode down the driveway laughing.

Brock hurried behind observing his leader from a safe distance. He prepared for quick action in case of the unexpected. He wondered why he had been so concerned over Justin's whereabouts. He was caught up in another one of Galley's great plans.

Two blocks later, Justin parked in front of a hedge near a front lawn. He hid the bike under some branches.

The canvas bag rubbed against Brock's shoulder blades. He dropped the packsack relieving the aching pressure. He waited further instructions.

Justin removed two cans of paint from the packsack. A shake of each hand set the scene in motion. "When I give a thumbs up get me more paint. When I point to the ground throw a handful of nails. Understood?"

"Nails! For what?"

Justin vanished without a word. He ran along a parked van and stopped at the hood of the vehicle. The tall boy raced around the van leaving a yellow trail. The can flew across the lawn. A second tin can rattled. Justin colored the doors, windows, hood, and tires red. He whipped the empty can across the grass. "Another one," the leader shouted.

Frightened by the outburst, Brock stood still. He waited for someone to appear. The street was bare and seemed safe. A paint can whirled through the air, landing at Justin's feet. The boy retrieved the can clenching his fist.

The leader raced to the next yard. A small bungalow occupied the property. A single car garage attached to the left side of the house.

Brock watched for movement. He rode past the house using

his guard's eyes. The bag rattled against his bike frame making him nervous. He secured the bag with his right hand and steered in a jerking motion with the left hand. A large rose bush presented the perfect hiding spot.

Justin maneuvered across the yard. He sneaked around an overgrown flowerbed creeping up to the garage. He pulled out artist tools required for his project.

Artistic shapes covered the brown door. Circles, squares, and lines raced from each stroke. The leader filled every spot with a jumping motion. His mark left a distinct message, which he admired in a proud curtsey.

Darkness fell over the neighborhood. Residents retired early and the street was quiet. Few bicycles and toys occupied Lively Road. As usual, Justin chose an area where victims were senior citizens.

The tall figure moved to the second house from the corner. Brock hurried across front lawns. He pedaled up to a fire hydrant, pausing for a street check. Streetlights dimmed overhead. The night was still. His bike rested against the red metal. Hunched over, he crept beside a wooden fence.

Justin waited at the end of the driveway. He pointed at the paved surface. The nail throwing episode terrified Brock. His leader beckoned but he shook his head repeatedly. The large boy pounced with both hands around his neck. "Throw the nails," he commanded.

Brock trembled. The packsack gained weight as his grip loosened. The ringleader shoved him forward. He stumbled to the ground. Brock's head rose in view of the truck. He crouched up the driveway, keeping low. The canvas stuck to his sweaty palms. He stopped behind the truck and looked back at his leader. Justin was gone. Brock double-checked and fled the scene. Suddenly, he fell backwards. His T-shirt tightened around his neck. He staggered into the vehicle. He looked up into enemy eyes. His ringleader stared down with daggers. Brock rubbed his neck and wiped his perspired face.

"Get off your butt and throw the nails, puppet."

Brock pulled himself up. He dropped a couple of nails at his feet. The leader yanked the packsack from his puppet. He pushed Brock aside. A large handful of spikes lifted from a deep compartment and pressed into Brock's hands.

"Throw them around the tires and underneath."

Sharp tips punctured the skin drawing blood on the palms of his hands. He held the nails tight squinting away the pain. He closed his eyes as the spikes flew. Nails chipped green paint from the side of the truck.

The big guy shouted, "Get out of the way."

Brock ran for his life. He never blinked until he curled up safe beside the fire hydrant. Escape crossed his mind but then someone shouted.

"Get away from there!"

Justin dashed across the property. Trailed by a yellow strip he climbed the four-foot picket fence, hurdling the top.

An elderly man shouted from the road, "You won't get away with this."

Justin leaped across the corner lot reaching his bike. A fast getaway led him down Glendale Road and right past the angry man. Justin weaved in front of Brock as they reached the corner. The two offenders raced back onto Lively and around the bend. The leader switched directions, turning onto Sandy Road. Brock pedaled full tilt behind his leader. Where was Justin headed, he thought.

Brock passed a small house on the corner and stopped. Justin was on someone's front lawn. He grabbed a 'No Trespassing' sign from the owner's property. "No one is telling me where I can go." He pulled the sign out of the ground and threw it against the brick home. He took nails from his pocket and bounced them down the driveway.

Nausea settled and Brock's abdominal muscles twisted. He looked around for a private spot when an elderly man shouted from the door, "Get out of here for the last time. I'm calling the police." The man rushed inside the house.

The word police scared Brock into instant vomit. His limbs weakened with clammy sweat. He had to get out of there fast but his stomach stalled his pace. He spotted Justin at the end of the street and pulled himself together to make his escape.

He used all the strength left in his legs to catch up with his leader. The race ended at the Statler house. Brakes slammed and Brock dropped his bike. He held his tightening chest. His shirt heaved in and out uncontrolled from fright and anger. Symptoms of a heart attack crossed his mind but he was more furious at Justin now.

The leader skidded to a halt. He bounced around, fully charged. "Boy, that guy was mad. Did you hear him yelling?"

Brock's legs wobbled as he approached Justin. Rage stormed inside but his stomach muscles strained, heaving all contents once again.

"I guess the excitement was too much for my puppet."

Brock straightened up and spilled his guts. "That was too close. That man saw you on Sandy Road. Was that the man who threatened to call the police on you before?"

Charged with excitement, Justin jumped around hysterically.

Brock took a deep breath to calm his rising temper. "Don't you understand anything? You added suspicion to yourself and still caused more trouble with Mr. Challens. It's bad enough that another person can identify you but I barely escaped again."

Justin shrugged. "What is the big deal? We got away didn't we?"

Hands squeezed together and Brock paced the cement. It was jump the big guy or try another approach. Grabbing Justin wasn't going to solve anything. "What's the matter with you? It is only time before the police pick you up, and judging from tonight I don't think it will be long from now. What will you do then? They only have a vague description of me but they can pick you out from a crowd."

"Aren't kids supposed to do what their parents tell them? My parents should be pleased with me after my good deed tonight."

The ringleader's smirk and restless behavior proved signs of trouble. Brock knew the night was young. "I don't think your dad meant destroying private property to show your talents. You should stay away from Mr. Challens."

Justin shared an evil stare. His voice deepened. "If you're so smart Statler, how did I get this scar?" He pointed at his face.

The mood swing ignited a time bomb, placing Brock in a danger zone. No warning came when Justin changed moods. He remembered the day he asked about the scar and was assured it was safer not answering this time.

The leader moved closer. Fierce eyes seeped inside of Brock. He searched for sensible words but Justin continued his details. "My old man threw me against the kitchen counter and ripped my face apart. I encountered our neighborhood blues for the first time during that visit. Old man Challens reported me and caused trouble between my dad and I."

Brock listened. The thought of any father acting like that was a shock. The zipper outlining Justin's face confirmed an act of violence. Brock sympathized. "If you don't want any trouble at home why bother Mr. Challens?"

"If it wasn't for that cantankerous old geezer I wouldn't be dodging blows to my head."

Brock lost his patience. "Justin, listen to what you are saying. Leave the man alone and you won't get into trouble. You would get along with your father and everything would be better." Brock paced the ground. He worked his frustration off and confronted his leader again. "What did Mr. Challens do to you tonight? Nothing, and you still took your actions out on him."

Justin overpowered Brock with a mean stare. He rested his hands on his hips. "You sound like my mom. I'm the one with the problem and everybody else is right. Let me clear the air, Statler. I'm not the one who needs a shrink. I've had it with you, my parents, and all of this town." Justin shoved Brock from his path and stomped away. His front wheel bounced up and down as he popped wheelies onto the road.

"You need help Justin."

The ringleader continued his fit of rage. Brock kicked the wheel on his bike. He hated talking to Justin because he never listened. He went into the house. Something strange confused Brock about his ringleader.

He escaped into his safe place for peace and quiet. Troubled thoughts unleashed in his workshop. His grandfather guided him through another difficult time.

"You can't judge a book by its cover," Grandpa always said.

Grandpa was right! Brock sat on his stool in the corner of his shop. He focused on his grandfather. *"Grandpa, I only know Justin from school and rumors from schoolmates. He is a class clown and can be trouble. I've seen what he is capable of."* Brock rubbed his chin. *"There has to be a logical reason for his temper flair ups and outbursts of anger. Why does Justin hate old people so much, Grandpa?"*

Brock believed in his grandfather and waited for a reply. It occurred that nobody took revenge on a person they didn't know. He read between the lines uncovering hidden facts.

"Grandpa, Justin resents Mr. Challens for reporting him but his anger stems from deeper within. I wonder if he knew the old man from years ago." Brock returned to his trance. He sharpened his detective skills and put his intuition to work. He believed more was at stake to the Galley's relationship with the old man. Justin's scar came to mind.

"I think Justin deserves a fair chance, Grandpa. Maybe he is abused at home or his real father abused him at one time. I don't think he has anyone to trust and that's why he has confided in me. Sometimes a stranger is easier to relate to than someone you know." Brock thought a friend was a good solution for Justin's problems.

The weekend sailed by with little social life. The birdhouse business expanded and occupied Brock's time. For the time being Justin remained in the background. Brock absorbed all the new skills possible as his dad explained procedures for checking belts, hoses, plugs, brakes and fuel systems. He found all his work overwhelming. Years of education supplied expertise from his dad in these procedures.

Friday night came. The clock ticked away as Brock waited for seven o'clock. The annual Northshore Summer Festival was a father and son event for the Statlers. This year brought a special surprise. Brock planned an all expense paid night for his dad. It was his treat because he was working. Nothing stood in the way of his night to remember. It was a piece of cake!

6

NIGHT OF TERROR

Brock cleared away the dinner dishes. He hurried into the living room where his dad watched the six o'clock news. The largest attraction began in Northshore. Brock counted the minutes for is big unveiling. He stood beside the lazy-boy chair waiting for the news to finish. At seven 'clock sharp he nudged his dad. "Ready to go?"

His father mumbled.

"What's that? I didn't hear you."

Interrupted by the doorbell Brock listened for his father's response as he left the living room. He peeked through a space in the opened door. Dressed in his best blue jeans and cut-off plaid shirt stood Justin Galley. It never dawned on Brock that his classmate would show up.

"What are you doing here?"

In a polite fashion, Justin replied, "Is that any way to greet a friend? I came to see if you wanted to go to the Summer Festival tonight."

Dad sneaked up behind Brock. "Who is it?"

Brock whispered, "It's Justin. I'll get rid of him." His visitor had opened the door.

"Come in Justin. Are you headed to the festival?" asked Mr. Statler.

"Yes sir. I stopped by to see if Brock wanted to go with me."

"My dad and I have plans for tonight." Brock noticed Justin's calm and well mannered approach. "I'm sorry Justin but we made plans weeks ago."

Dad cleared his throat. His voice softened. "Why don't you join your friend tonight Brock?"

"But Dad it's father and son night, remember."

His father blushed. "I have work to finish at the shop tonight. It will take at least two hours. No sense in both of us missing out on the fun."

Brock lowered his head. "It was supposed to be our time together. We never miss the Northshore Summer Festival."

"I'm sorry son. An emergency came up and there is no way out of it." Dad nodded at Justin. "You boys will have more fun without an adult hanging around."

Heart broken Brock replied, "Okay Dad. I know work comes first. I'll see you when you get home."

The boys left the house and Brock snapped. "I hope you realize I had a fabulous surprise for my dad tonight."

"It's a good job I came by or you would be sitting at home alone."

"This is the way it's going to be tonight. We go to the festival as friends but no funny stuff. That means no pranks or stunts. We act like buddies instead of criminals. Got it?"

Justin winked. Brock ignored the doubts running through his mind in exchange for a normal evening. He rode away without another word.

Twenty minutes passed in silence. The Summer Festival opened its arms with colored lights flashing above the

activities. Crowds rushed for the rides. People pushed in line-
ups. The festival grounds led along Centennial Drive to the
waterfront. Police patrolled the blocked off intersections. They
directed cars into parking areas and prevented motorists from
entering the fair grounds. Parked vehicles sandwiched together
on both sides of the streets. Thousands of Northshore residents
and hundreds of out of town visitors supported the annual
event. Bikes locked at a cement barricade at the main entrance.

Justin and Brock strolled through the ride section passing
the Ferris wheel, bumper cars, swings, and roller coaster. Brock
shivered seeing the swings. Watching the circular motion made
him dizzy. "That's one ride you'll never catch me on. I'm afraid
the strap will let go and shoot me into orbit."

Justin giggled. "Chicken! These rides are kid's stuff."

Ticket booths set up between the rides. Anxious children
waited while parents bought tickets. Crowds mushroomed
stretching lines of people out at the gates. Speakers blared
music situated around the rides. Teenagers screamed as the
swings suspended them in mid air.

"Where do you want to go first?" Brock shouted.

Justin pointed at the tents. "Let's check out the target
games."

The leader stopped at the dart-throwing tent and Brock
checked the surrounding area. The same games appeared year
after year. Target booths included throwing darts, baseballs,
hard balls, or beanbags. Prizes covered the back wall and hung
down both sides of each tent. Prizes ranged from four-inch
stuffed animals to large five-foot ones. Small plastic toys drew
attention for younger children.

Signs displayed assorted soft drinks, cotton candy, and
smothered buttered popcorn. Brocks stomach growled for the
buttered popcorn. It was time to eat. Justin disappeared from

the dart target so Brock searched the food prospects.

Colored balloons stood in large round containers outside various vendors. Cartoons doodled over them with different sayings. Children created their own candles at the next tent. Another vendor displayed colored sand ornaments. A variety of shaped glassware contained layered sand. A stick pushed colors down the sides of the container mixing the sand together. The finished project created rainbow designs through the glass container.

Bang! Bang! Brock spun around. The racket came from his leader. Destruction marked the scene. A lit cigarette stuck out of his hand. He made eye contact and grinned. Another balloon hanging from the bean toss tent popped. *Bang! Bang,* went a third balloon.

Brock ignored Justin. He sneaked between adults passing by and followed into a clearing. The festival grounds separated into the next phase of activities. Over one hundred tents connected and crowds mingled around the vendors. People scattered everywhere. Tents spread out across the open area. Less activity took place on this side. Overwhelmed by the number of vendors displaying merchandise, Brock checked each tent along the way. Vendors sold clothing, ceramics, crafts, jewelry, candy, and candles. Customers viewed knitting, sewing, toys, and woodworking. Customers heard their fortunes told by a woman with a crystal ball.

Food vendors situated everywhere. Brock sniffed hotdogs and hamburgers from near by grills. Deep fried foods lingered in the evening air. Pizza followed scents of lasagna, spaghetti, and chili. The mild summer breeze floated golden fries and onion rings his way. Mixed aromas created hunger. The sight of food dried out Brock's mouth. He stepped up to the window of an ice cream trailer.

"May I help you?" asked a young woman.

So many flavors made a difficult decision. Brock licked his lips tasting the flavors. He chose his favourite ice cream. "I would like a chocolate chip ice-cream cone please." Seconds later he paid for his treat and savored every bite. Cold chocolate melted down his throat. He chewed bits of chocolate chips washing them down with the soft ice cream.

Someone tapped his shoulder. Brock shoved his cone into his face. Chocolate smeared all over his nose and mouth.

"Hungry Statler? There's a great pepperoni pizza with our name on it just across the way."

Brock wiped his face on a napkin. He looked around the grounds but didn't see anyone chasing Justin. Relieved he licked the cone again. "Sure. Give me a second to finish this."

The leader slapped his back and headed for the pizza booth. Brock devoured the last mouthful of cone when he stepped in line behind his friend. The dark hair teenager moved beside Brock. "You order and I'll be right back."

"Still want the pepperoni?"

Justin yelled over his shoulder, "Doesn't matter."

Pepperoni floated around the tent. Brock craved for a bite of his specialty.

"What would you like?" asked an elderly man.

"I'll have two pieces of pepperoni with extra cheese and a side order of garlic bread."

Brock bobbed up and down looking for Justin. He wondered what happened to his classmate. His hand covered his stomach controlling fierce growls. He skipped dinner to eat at the festival.

"Your order is ready, son."

Brock paid for the meal and went around the tent in search of his leader. The steaming pizza absorbed heat through the paper napkin. He feared dropping it. An empty picnic table caught his attention.

"Over here," someone called.

Justin strolled over to Brock with two beverages raised above his head. "Just what the doctor ordered, right pal?" He handed him an orange soda.

Pop cases stacked behind the Pizza tent grabbed Brock's attention. He backed away, waving his hands.

"No way. You didn't!"

"What if I did? You want me to put yours back?" Justin turned to leave.

Brock stomped across the grass. He remembered the hot pizza in his hands and marched back to Justin. Hot pepperoni and cheese tossed at the leader's chest. "The pizza is also free. I don't believe you. I actually thought we could have fun tonight. You acted normal, earlier." Brock headed for the picnic table under the pine trees.

Justin chased after him. "Don't be such a poor sport. Wait up!"

Brock blocked out the nuisance and sat on the bench. He dug into the cheese and pepperoni enjoying his meal. He bit into the delicious garlic bread.

Justin leaned over his puppet's shoulder. "Are you mad?"

Anger diminished Brock's appetite. Money tossed into the garbage was waste so he wrapped up the leftovers to take home. Clenched fists aimed at the big guy before he realized his actions. He slammed his fists into his lap. "How do you act innocent one minute and a terrorist the next? You are forever changing moods."

"That's me! I'm unpredictable and full of surprises. You wanted lots of excitement and adventure over the summer and now it's too much to handle."

"We seem to have different opinions about adventure. I'll stick with my excitement. I think it's safer and legal that way."

A hand grabbed his arm. Justin tilted his head in a shy manner. "You like animals?"

Brock nodded.

Justin released his hold. "Let's go to the petting zoo. We can feed the animals."

The petting zoo spread out on the other side of the country talent show. A large open stage presented local talent. Singers performed songs by favourite artists and the winners received awards while some had future singing careers. People gathered over the rough grounds. Lawn chairs sat in rows, circles, or alone. Young and old listened to the country hits.

Brock listened to the music. Loud clapping from the audience drowned out clarity of the words. Favourite singers from previous years drew greatest attention.

Justin sighed. "This is boring."

"See what I mean. You can't stand still for a couple of minutes and you're bored. Don't your parents listen to country music?"

"How should I know? I'm not home at nights and my mom sleeps most days. I don't know what they listen to. I like rap music myself."

"Do you get along with your mom?"

Justin swung around. "I get enough third degree at home, Statler."

Brock cautioned his line of questioning. "You never talk about your mother. I was curious, that's all." He hesitated. "Just to be sure we are clear on one thing, you pull another stunt, I'm gone. Got it?" The weird smirk bothered Brock but he refused to let it spoil his night.

The petting zoo spread off to the right over a flat field.

Clouds covered the blue sky and darkness hovered. Dampness settled in the air.

"Let's feed the animals and head back."

Justin rushed to the fence. "Come on they have cones filled with feed. Look, they're only a dollar a piece."

The leader's face lit up like a little kid. He paid the looney and raced inside the pen. A first visit at a petting zoo brought such excitement and it pleased Brock to see his friend having fun for a change. He felt sorry because Justin wasn't aware of events going on in the community. It seemed he never attended any social functions before.

The fenced pen had only a couple of visitors. Justin held out his hand to a tall woolly llama. A strange sight appeared seeing something hovering over the big guy. Everyone he knew was shorter than Justin.

Brock bought two cones of feed and headed for a silky brown fawn. It stood alone at the far end of the pens. He crept towards the shy baby. He gestured the innocent fawn closer watching him nibble at the cone. Brock glanced around the open pens. Sheep and goats balked from strangers. Chickens, roosters and hens darted under moving feet. Two llamas patrolled the passages. Pigs squealed and ponies flicked their heads for attention. Manure and droppings were unpleasant to endure but it came with the territory.

Brock acquainted himself with a miniature black pony. He observed new visitors in the small fenced area. Someone screamed. He stepped backwards into a warm squishy pile of manure from his mare friend. Brock scuffed his joggers on the ground to remove the build up. Straw stuck to the bottom of his shoes and made it impossible to rub off.

Commotion came from the gate. Llamas, goats, and chickens scurried in terror. The gate attendant chased the loose pets. Young children cried and older ones screamed with laughter. Brock raced through the obstacle course to get outside the fence. He dragged his feet trying to clean his shoes at the same time. Adults grabbed children and darted for safety. A man in uniform raced after the larger animals. Brock noticed Justin bent over in laughter. He hid behind the wooden fence pointing at the loose herd.

Brock escaped the turmoil and continued past his leader. He stopped at the closest curb to scrape his joggers clean. Justin caught up at the first set of tents and grabbed Brock. "Did you see how happy those animals were to be free?"

Brock loosened the grip and pulled away. "Can't you go anywhere without causing a disturbance. I guess I was wrong about us hanging out as friends. You have one thing on your mind at all times and I don't want to be anywhere near it."

"What do you mean? We hang out all the time Statler. What's the big deal about having some fun?"

"The Night Hawks hang out, not friends. I've had enough with your so-called fun. You do what makes you happy and I'll make sure I'm as far away as possible." Brock detoured for the next set of tents.

The leather vendor was the first tent on the corner. He eased between racks searching for the special gift. He checked each item carefully and focused on finding the leather belt his dad admired last year. His father browsed the tents every year and never bought himself anything.

Brock found the belt rack. He spun the metal around. A soft leather belt with hand carved workmanship along the middle strip and a square buckle stood out with pride. It was his father's belt.

He marched over to the owner and set the belt on the counter. "I'll take this one."

"Fine choice. That will be twenty dollars," said the man.

Brock paid for the gift and put his left over meal into the same bag. He tucked the bag under his arm and left a satisfied customer.

The sky darkened in seconds. Ride lights lit up some sections of the grounds. Dim shadows covered most areas and Brock judged his footing with care. It took more time than he expected to shop. Nighttime gathered more adults over the festival grounds. He struggled through the crowds, which forced him to go around circles joined in conversation.

Brock's night ended and he headed for the main entrance. Lights blinded him at the ride section. Music roared above noisy crowds. Activity intensified as rides filled. Adults and teenagers deafened the ears with shrilling screams.

He continued between the bumper cars and swings. A distant noise startled him. He stretched his neck in view over a young couple ahead of him. People passed back and forth. He bobbed between bodies but nothing stood out. Someone called. He peeked through oncoming crowds the second time. Arms waved overhead in the distance.

"Statler over here."

Brock crossed to the swings and discovered Justin. The leader leaned against a power supply box next to the Ferris wheel. A huge grin spread across his face. He waved Brock closer.

"Oh, no!" Gasped Brock. Chills tingled up his spine. He panicked at the large plugs connected to the electrical panel. He stayed at the metal fence surrounding the swings. Nobody suspected anything.

Justin pulled a thick black plug from the electrical box. Brock froze. He closed his eyes for a split second. The Ferris wheel lights shut off filling the area with blackness. His legs wouldn't budge. He turned into a statue. Silence escaped his lungs. Another plug popped. The large wheel stopped in mid air. Justin yanked the plugs one after another. Riders screamed in terror. Panic shrieked over the grounds like a blaze out of control. Adult feet vibrated the surface assisting in rescue. Ride attendants shouted for help increasing the turmoil. Security guards multiplied and a nightmare born.

Men, women and children shoved into the midst of action. The large wheel caged horrified passengers to their seats. Frightened teenagers lost their dinners, stirring up more commotion. Minutes turned the fair grounds into a disaster. Brock snapped out of his trance and ran for the road. He tripped over a thick-coated wire, connected to one of the rides. Justin knocked him off balance as he shot past him.

"Get that kid."

Brock scrambled to his feet. Three police officers headed his way. He ran full speed ahead. His heart pounded. His legs numbed. The pavement guided him to the cement blockade. Sweaty palms fumbled the lock on his bike. It was stuck. Brock turned to shouting voices approaching. He jiggled the lock with shaking fingers until it fell. He jolted the frame free, plunking himself hard onto his seat.

Justin was out of sight and Brock pedaled vigorously. Every inch of muscle worked overtime. His strength increased as home gained on him. Tears welcomed his neighborhood. Safety pressured him onto Princeton Avenue and Brock continued with fright.

The dim streetlight revealed a tall shadow at the end of his driveway. Distance shortened along with his temper. Anger reached boiling point at the sight of Justin. Brock slammed on his brakes ramming into the ten-speed. He sprung from his bike grabbing the leader by the shoulders. "What in the world were you doing? Those people were terrified."

"What's the matter with you, Statler?" Justin shook himself free. "That was the greatest rush ever. More excitement than you'll ever get on those rides."

Brock punched at his leader's chest, "You could have killed someone. That was the most dangerous and irresponsible thing I've ever witnessed. You need serious help Justin. You're going to hurt someone, if not kill them." Brock trembled with rage. He walked away from his leader before he punched him again.

Justin attacked. "Don't tell me what to do puppet. Remember, you do what I say." He slammed his fists into the handlebars. "This is what the Night Hawks stand for. You are one of us whether you like it or not, Statler."

Brock grabbed his bike. "I am not a member of your gang. I will not terrorize innocent people and your puppet just died, so find yourself another one. Better still, why don't you forget about the Night Hawks. They are only a figment of your imagination. Try handling problems the realistic way for a change."

Justin kicked his wheel and yelled, "Don't walk away from me puppet. You owe me, Statler. The Night Hawks are real and we look after ourselves. You can't quit until I say so."

"I owe you nothing. Maybe you do need a shrink. Sounds like your problems are getting worse. I thought being a friend would make you open up but that doesn't seem to work."

Justin mumbled and raced off in a rage.

Brock disappeared downstairs when he realized his father wasn't home from work. It gave him space to think on his terms. Fear swallowed his insides. Brock cried at his workbench. He covered his face releasing loud sobs. Horror spilled out in shame. He confided in his special listener.

"Grandpa, I was so angry tonight. I shouldn't have said what I did. Please forgive me for losing it with Justin." He sobbed and continued, *"I witnessed the most terrifying thing in my life tonight and people could have died. I panicked instead of preventing the horror that took place at the festival. What have I done? Forgive me Grandpa for selfish changes I've made with my life. I've turned into an evil monster."*

Brock felt somewhat relieved getting his thoughts off his chest. His mentor helped him find solutions. He took a giant step tonight and confronted Justin head on. Courage ended his membership in the Night Hawks.

The back door closed. Brock wiped his face and made an escape for the bedroom. His dad ran into him in the hallway.

"Hi son. How was your night?"

"Okay. How was work?"

Dad poured a glass of milk. "Busy as usual but the rush is over. Trenton called after you left. He was sorry he missed you and will see you Labor Day Weekend."

"I would have stayed home if I knew he was calling." Brock dropped his elbows onto the counter sinking his face into his hands.

Dad finished his drink and sat at the table. "Labor Day Weekend will be here before you know it. Cheer up, son. You have lots to occupy yourself until then."

"I know, only five more weeks to go. It seems ages since Trenton was here." Brock yawned and waved goodnight. "It's been a long day. I'm going to bed."

Snuggled under cozy blankets he shut out the night and the nightmare he witnessed. He prayed for Tuesday morning when he would be working. The Night Hawks overpowered his thoughts even in the comfort of his bed. Brock's nightmare also woke the following day.

7

UNDERCOVER ANGEL

Brock pushed the shop broom across the concrete floor. Sand and dirt piled up around the shop. He ran into stacked containers in the corner, knocking them over. He paid no attention and continued sweeping.

"Brock," called his dad.

The oversize broom dragged behind Brock. Work boots thumped with each step as he crossed the shop to his father. "You want me, Dad?"

His father seemed puzzled about something. "Are you all right, son?"

"I guess so."

"Either your mind is not on work, or you dislike those containers." Dad pointed to the corner.

A cloud surrounded Brock distracting him with distant voices. Confusion bothered him.

Dad crossed his arms leaned against his tool chest and studied Brock for a few seconds.

"Anything new at the Summer Festival?"

The festival played non-stop in Brock's mind. He dreamt

about the horror taken place that evening. A girl hanging from a Ferris wheel haunted him. She screamed for help but no one came. The thought turned his blood cold.

"What's the matter, Brock?"

Once again he lied. "The festival wasn't the same without you, Dad. I planned to treat you to a night out." He covered his mouth remembering that his dad's gift sat on his dresser. "I have a surprise for you after work."

Dad squeezed Brock's shoulders and whispered, "There is always next year to take me out. I promise to keep that weekend free."

Brock grinned and threw his dad a high five. "Sounds like a date."

The morning sailed by. After he cleaned the shop, Brock sorted his dad's tools. He arranged screwdrivers, pliers, and wrenches in their proper places. He took out the garbage and picked up scraps in the back lot.

Dad worked on a jeep with another mechanic. Brock's hands slipped on the greasy surface as he peeked under the hood. His nose twitched from the cleaner sitting beside the vehicle.

"Ready for an oil change, son?"

Brock rubbed his hands. "Sure!"

"First of all, you see that cap there. That's the oil filler cap. Unscrew it with the wrench and remove the cap from the valve cover."

Brock removed the oil filler cap. "Why do you take that off?"

"The air has to flow through while the oil drains out." Dad pointed at Brocks feet. "Now take that pan and put it underneath the front end."

Brock laid flat on the crawler. The wooden surface hurt his

back. He pushed his hands and rolled backwards using his feet. He aimed under the jeep.

"Place the pan under the engine where the oil pan is. See the metal plug from the oil pan?"

"Got yah, Dad."

"Unscrew the plug and pull it out. The oil will run into the pan on the floor."

The plug pulled out. "Yuck!" Brock crawled out from under the vehicle.

Dad laughed. "Forgot to mention to keep your face away when you pull the plug. Guess you know now."

Brock wiped his face with a rag, smearing the substance over his skin. A slippery coating remained on his face. The extra layer of skin sealed dirt into place. Oil wasn't as bad as gas fumes and Brock didn't mind the facial. "What's next?"

Dad pointed inside the hood. "See that metal object shaped like a tube beside the engine?"

"What's that?"

"That is your filter. Unscrew the filter with the wrench and we'll replace it with a new one."

Brock took out the dirty filter while his dad brought him a new one. He screwed in the new filter. A shove of his heels positioned him underneath the jeep. He screwed the plug back into the oil pan.

"Now son, pour new oil and check to make sure it is full."

Brock shrugged. "How do I know how many liters this takes, and how do I check it?"

Dad grinned. "Most vehicles take four liters but if you're not sure take the dipstick and stick it down inside. When you pull the dipstick out it will mark the level of oil."

"Is that all?" laughed Brock.

The large clock on the wall told his dad it was almost

lunchtime. "Don't forget to screw the oil filler cap back onto the valve cover. After you're finished here, pick up the containers in the corner and then it is break time."

Brock saluted and finished his oil change. He looked into the cracked mirror hanging on the far wall. He rubbed his face with a dirty rag. It was hard distinguishing between oil on his face or smudges on the glass.

He piled the containers one at a time and stacked the last one. The garage door slammed. Mechanics twisted their heads to the loud bang. A second look assured Brock he wasn't dreaming. Arms swung with marching steps. A red face and devilish eyes announced rampage. Brock slid behind a stack of new tires but Justin headed straight for him.

"We have unfinished business and this time there won't be any evidence left."

Brock peeked around the tires. His dad and the other employees watched. Justin's rough voice carried for all to hear. "Keep your voice down. What's this about evidence?"

The big guy squished Brock against the wall. He jabbed him in the chest while he spoke.

"Challens did it this time. I have to shut him up for good and you are going to be my witness."

The concrete scraped Brock's back. He managed to shake his head. "No! I'm out of this."

Justin produced the slack needed and Brock shoved the leader aside. The leader grabbed the front of his gray work shirt, lifting him into the air. Brock dangled like a puppet on a string. The cotton material tightened across his windpipe. Blood rushed to his head with increased body temperature. Heavy steel-toed boots slapped onto concrete. Brock stood in the open area embarrassed by observing eyes.

Justin lifted the shirt tighter, looking square into his

puppet's eyes. "Meet me at the corner of Baker and Martin tonight at eight o'clock sharp. Just remember, Statler, my problem ends tonight, but yours could begin if you don't show. Nothing says I can't take care of two problems at the same time."

Dad stepped forward and Brock blurted, "I'll be there."

His shirt loosened. Justin hurried off slamming the door. Brock's throat scratched as he swallowed. He concentrated on the closed door. His face heated and dizziness swarmed his head. He ignored the stares wishing he could massage his sore throat. He was certain everyone overheard his conversation.

Dad announced lunch break and the three employees took their regular spots. Brock picked up his metal lunch pail and went to his father. He focused on the pail in his hand. "Dad, do you think I could take the afternoon off?"

His father shifted sideways on a wooden crate, prolonging his answer. "No problem. Do you need help with anything?" Dad gestured at the door.

"Not now."

"Get rested up for a fresh start in the morning. I'll pick dinner up on my way home."

Brock left the shop in silence. He spent the afternoon deep in thought. Time flew by with no progress in sight. Curled up on the couch he held a picture of an aging man. The wide smile reached out to him. A special bond offered assistance. Brock felt close to his grandfather at that moment and his troubles poured out as he looked into the caring face.

"I'm in big trouble. I thought Justin would stop involving me in his pranks if I quit the Night Hawks. He's determined to get even with Mr. Challens. I don't know the man, only to see him, but I feel something terrible is going to happen."

Brock rubbed his chin remembering his grandfather's

friend, Mr. Thomas. He was an elderly man whom teenagers terrorized early in the evenings. Grandpa took his night walks later so he could check on Mr. Thomas. The neighborhood teenagers stopped bothering the man when they knew he wasn't alone.

His grandfather stared back from the frame. *"Mr. Challens is in danger and needs protection."* Brock thought about his choices. *"I could report Justin to the police but that would implicate me. I can only come up with one solution, Grandpa. I believe a witness has more opportunity to protect someone in trouble. As long as I am nearby nothing will happen to Mr. Challens."*

He looked into the colored photograph and studied his grandfather's expression. Brock jumped from the couch hugging the picture. *"Thank you Grandpa. I knew you would agree."*

Brock solved his problem to satisfaction. He glanced at the clock above the television set. It was dinner. The old truck rumbled into the yard. The back door closed and his father chanted, *"Kentucky Fried Chicken, special delivery from the Colonel."*

Brock rushed into the kitchen. Deep-fried chicken called his growling stomach. Dad pulled out a ten piece chicken dinner. He reached for the next bag but it was gone. Brock snatched it out from under his dad's nose.

"Slow down there, son. There's plenty of food."

"Let me help. I'm starving." Brock dove into the paper bag, retrieving all contents. "Mm, golden fries and my favourite macaroni salad."

"You must be hungry, it's a good thing we don't have to cook it first." Dad smiled and handed a plate to Brock.

He loaded fries, a crispy chicken leg, and a large crunchy

breast onto his plate. He sniffed the delicious scent. A large piece of skin stuffed into his mouth letting juices run down his chin. He chewed until his mouth was empty. "This tastes as good as it smells."

Dad fixed his plate and joined Brock at the dinner table. "Having the afternoon off must have been what the doctor ordered."

Brock smiled. He squeezed the ketchup bottle, coating his fries red. Long strips of crinkled potatoes slid into his mouth one at a time. A tall glass of cold milk washed down his meal.

After dinner, Brock pushed his plate aside settling back in his chair. He exchanged looks with his father.

"Something on your mind, son?"

Brock cleared his throat before he spoke. "Dad do you believe in angels?"

"Yes."

"A guardian angel protects someone while they are living, right?"

"Yes, everyone has a guardian angel who watches over them," answered Dad.

"Can a person be a guardian angel on earth?" Brock regretted his question as soon as his father scratched his unshaven chin and squinted. He went too far on this subject.

"If you help people and do good things during your life, that is like being an angel on earth."

His father's puzzled expression told Brock it was time for an explanation. He wiggled on the wooden seat, straightened in his chair, and proceeded. "Dad what does a person do when they know someone is in danger?"

His father leaned forward. He seemed awkward about answering. "That's a big question, son. It depends on the danger involved. If the person were frightened, it would be a concern."

"What if something serious was going to happen but nobody knew what it was?"

"That person should tell someone what was happening, contact proper authorities, and let them handle it." Dad folded his arms as he leaned back in his seat. He looked funny. "What does this have to do with guardian angels?"

Brock hesitated. He stuttered, "No...nothing to do...with angels."

His father frowned. "Does Justin have anything to do with these questions?"

Brock scraped off his plate. How was he to tell his father he had to save an innocent man from a maniac teenager? How was his father going to understand his motive for being an angel? Brock refused to face the tall man standing behind him.

"No. Just wondered about some stuff, that's all."

Dad put his dinner dishes on the counter. "I'm going to catch the last few minutes of the news. Want to join me Brock?"

"I have some cleaning downstairs and then I'm going out for a bit."

Brock picked up wood scraps, cleaned brushes, and made a list of supplies. He promised a complete list by Friday. It was pay week and meant more supplies. He organized his agenda for the rest of the week. He completed his business and another type of business followed. It was meeting time.

Tension rose at the corner of Martin Street and Baker. Brock prayed Justin wouldn't show, but his prayers were missed. The leader of the Night Hawks barreled around the corner.

"Glad you showed up, Statler. That's a point in your favor."

Brock kept silent.

"The cops gave me a final warning Friday night and now it's my turn to relate a warning."

"What did you get caught for now?"

Justin twisted the rubber handles on his bike. He fumbled with the pedals. "I paid a visit to Challens. The cops showed up threatening to lay charges next time." Justin slammed his fists into the metal frame. "My old man took the cop's side. He's threatened to kick me out if the blues come knocking one more time."

Brock showed no emotion as his leader blew up.

"Can you believe my own father throwing me out? That old man is going to pay big time and there won't be anything tying me to the crime."

Sweat soaked Brock's shirt against his chest. He wiped his hands down the leg of his shorts. "Sounds pretty serious. Don't you think it is time to stop blaming this man for your trouble?" His voice cracked.

Justin pointed at Brock. "The game isn't over until I say so. That's where my puppet comes in."

A dry cough scraped the back of Brock's throat. Moisture released from all pores. A flashback reminded him to act casual. This was his chance to protect one of Justin's victims from his cruel revenge. "I'm not a hit man and won't take part in hurting someone." Brock swallowed the lump in his throat. "What do you want from me, Justin?"

The leader sprung off his bike. Brock gripped his handles for security. He jerked his head away expecting a punch. Instead, a long finger poked his face.

"Your job is to be here tomorrow night at eight-thirty. I will take care of business. You will make sure nobody identifies us. Tomorrow night the puppet will witness a pro at work." The leader's hysterical laugh escaped, once again.

"What do you mean identify us? What's the plan?"

An evil smirk crossed Justin's face. He waved his hands

back and forth. "No plan, Statler. Just show up as watchman. You're in for the surprise of your life." The leader laughed.

The high pitched sound scared Brock. It wasn't natural. He yelled, "Wait! I need to know details."

"That's all the puppet needs to know. Just be at this corner."

Justin was capable of anything and that terrified Brock. Fear of the unknown weakened the puppet. His previous plan as guardian angel presented doubts. Time came to cut the puppet strings.

8

DEADLY REVENGE

Signs of autumn bloomed the first week of August. The sun lowered its head for the night. A chill set over Northshore after a day of warm temperatures.

Eight thirty arrived with the onset of jitters. Brock journeyed to meet his leader. He extended his ride as long as possible. Discolored leaves scattered on a corner lot. He imagined floating weightless with no worries in the world. Summer ended in four weeks and Brock's best friend entered his mind.

A tall figure slumped over a ten-speed. The leader waited for his puppet. Brock rode up beside the new bike. He took a deep breath and planted both feet. The thick air released danger.

"What did you do to Mr. Challens Friday night? You never told me what happened."

Stretched back on his seat, the ringleader smirked. "I exploded. You talked back to me after the Summer Festival and no one ever talked to me like that." Justin flung his arms. "The cops brainwashed my old man and now he wants to put me away." A clenched fist smacked into the palm of his hand. A tightened jaw stretched the zipper teeth along Justin's cheek.

Brock shuddered at grinding teeth. He phrased careful words. "Why did you go after the old man if I made you mad? Why didn't you come after me?"

"The old man was an easy target. I have plans for you. You'll regret your words, puppet."

"I told the truth. You need some help, Justin. Why are you doing this to a senior citizen? What is the point of pestering someone, anyway?"

Justin exposed the side of his face revealing his left eye. "That's why, Statler."

The swollen black eye wasn't there last night. It was a whopper. Brock was tongue-tied. Maybe this guy had told the truth about his father. Someone had beaten Justin. Goose bumps popped out all over Brock's arms. He quivered at the thought of anyone hitting him that hard.

"See my point?" continued Justin. "Cops suspect me in the neighborhood vandalism but they don't have solid proof. This was my old man's way of keeping an eye on me." He pointed at the shiner. "Challens isn't getting the last laugh. We have a job to finish." Justin took the lead, waving his puppet onward.

"Wait!" yelled Brock. "What are you going to do?"

Justin kept going. Brock followed into the unknown night. A short distance felt like eternity. Spaced far enough behind the leader Brock reassured his plan of action. Somehow, bravery felt wrong at this point. He focused on the important issue at hand, saving a human life.

A small gray bungalow appeared on the corner of Sandy Road. A large full-grown hedge sheltered the side and front of the small yard. A paved drive led up to a carport. Flowerbeds showcased the front windows, down the sidewalk, and designed the front landscape. Retired couples were major occupants in the quiet area.

A trail led alongside Mr. Challens driveway. Justin took this same path to school each day. A bolder blocked the center portion of the entrance. Space was left on each side of the large stone. Overgrown bush enveloped the sides of the path leaving little room.

Justin dropped his bike behind the six-foot enclosure. The cedar hedge protected him. Something was odd! The leader had no packsack for this prank. The tall figure searched the premises. Nobody was in sight. The house seemed dark but a small hatchback sat in the driveway. The old man was home.

Justin whistled. Brock closed in behind the cedars.

"You are a witness. Don't say or do anything. Whistle if you spot intruders and watch a creative mind in action. When the job is done, make sure nothing is left for evidence. Last of all, tell me who got the last laugh." Laughter roared as the leader slapped Brock on the back.

Chills sneaked up and down his spine. His partner in crime was a sick guy. His behavior was out of control. Brock prayed for a safe ending to the night. He asked for any sign letting him know when and what action was required.

The tall boy crouched along the hedges and disappeared. Rattled noises came from the carport. Two metal garbage cans rolled down the driveway. One bounced onto the front lawn spilling garbage. The front porch light flickered on. The light went off seconds later. Justin picked up the tin on the lawn and ran around spreading garbage all over. He dumped food scraps and paper across the tidy lawn. The empty metal can flew into the driveway. The leader raced for the second garbage can. Recycled tins, cardboard, and jars soared in all directions. Glass crashed against pavement.

Brock covered his ears. Danger crept through the yard. His limbs weakened with fright. A fast check confirmed a deserted street. Dark clouds brewed a storm as temperatures dropped. Moist air doomed near by rain.

The front light brightened up the yard. The door swung open. Seconds later blackness swept over the porch. Mr. Challens stepped out onto the platform and mumbled. The man moved around on the step. A coarse voice yelled, "Who's there? What is going on?"

No one answered. Brock covered his mouth. He was positive the man saw the mess on the lawn. A scuffle sounded and the door slammed. Either the light burned out before he noticed the garbage or the man wasn't wearing his glasses, thought Brock.

Justin jumped out from the carport holding a long garden hose. He dragged the green snake below the large bay window. Sheltered by the living room window, he pressed the nozzle down spraying full force against the glass. He ran along the front of the brick home. He soaked the roof, windows, and flowerbeds. Pressure aimed at the front door made a terrible racket. The leader dashed out of sight when the door opened. Mr. Challens stayed inside the house. He peeked out and closed the door.

Justin vanished. Silence fell over the property. A noise alerted Brock. He looked around the yard. Nothing was there. Something flew past the hedge. He stretched his neck, seeing plants scattered all over the front lawn. Soggy flowers tossed everywhere and flowerbeds destroyed. Small shrubs remained alone.

The tall figure disappeared again. Brock kept a watchful eye. Metal screeched. Scratching sounds came from the house. He squinted. Something moved near the corner of the house. The ringleader clasped a long handled shovel between his hands. The round mouth scraped the basement concrete. Justin staggered towards the flowerbed. He dug small shrubs and rose bushes. He pitched loose ones over his shoulder. The shovel split shrubs apart. Grey bricks scraped as the leader marched along the front of the house. The door opened a crack. Justin ran for cover and waited beside the porch.

Brock squatted between openings in the hedge. He covered his eyes at such cruel behavior. He prayed his guardian to send a sign. Time came for his stand. He opened his eyes when the door opened. Mr. Challens life depended on his quick actions.

Justin banged the shovel against the brick. He hit the porch railing vibrating the metal bar. The light turned on and a tall heavyset man appeared in the doorway. His silver streaked hair glistened in the porch light. He remained inside the doorframe. "Who's there?"

A shrub sprung out of nowhere. It hit the door casing causing the man to leap out of the way. A rough voice sounded, "I know you're there. Stop this right now."

The light went off and the door closed. Brock crept closer to the house. Shadows limited his view from the dim streetlights. A loud bang exploded from the rear property. *Crash!* The branches separated as Justin barreled around the corner of the house. A shovel extended over his head. The door opened. Justin raised the shovel high in view. Brock leaped from the cedars as the shovel swung at the door. He dashed into the open concentrating on lighted areas. A faint glimpse of the leader showed through the light. Mr. Challens stepped onto the platform. Brock held his breath as the shovel swung through the air.

Without hesitation Brock shouted, "Look out!"

The old man jumped to the left. The shovel hit the wall. Justin swung harder the second time.

Brock screamed, "No Justin. No!"

Mr. Challens lost his balance falling into the corner of the door. The shovel swiped past the man's body crashing into the railing. The old man crawled into the house and the door closed. Justin raced to the hedges. Stunned by the commotion, Brock fell to the ground. Fists punched and knuckles jabbed his chest and face. A blow to the head shocked him. Pain rushed from one side of his head to the other. Limited strength prevented him from fighting back.

Justin repeated, "Stupid, stupid Statler. You're going to pay for this. I could have had the old geezer and you screwed it big time."

Sirens squealed in the distance. "You hear that?" said Brock.

Red lights flashed, as sirens grew louder. An ambulance and two police cruisers sped up the road. "Police!" shouted Brock.

Justin pushed himself off his puppet and hid behind the bushes. Brock escaped through neighborhood yards. His body ached as he raced for his life. Houses, trees, and vehicles passed in a blur. A worn out frame carried him to the safety of his home.

Brock slipped through the back door hiding out in the washroom. His head pounded. He held trembling hands and looked into the mirror. A thin face spotted with dirt and fresh blood looked back at him. Warm liquid ran down his pale face. Cheekbones swelled under puffy blue eyes. He panicked at the stranger peering back.

Brock washed away the visual evidence. Pain in his heart was internal baggage he had to deal with in time. He went to his room and dropped onto his bed. He prayed that his grandfather watched over him in his time of need.

"I saved a man's life tonight but I don't feel good about myself. Something is wrong because the police and paramedics

came. I did my best, Grandpa. One look at my face will lead Dad to a third degree. I don't know whether to lie or be honest. I've lied too many times and it hurts."

Brock contemplated the truth over reliving events of the past month. Exhaustion took priority and solutions waited for a clearer analysis.

Aches reminded Brock of last night's episode. His stiff body jerked with every movement causing a throbbing headache. His dad moved around in the kitchen so a detour to the bathroom was safe.

The stranger reappeared. Puffed eyes replayed last night's fight. Brock wasn't bruised but a cut lip was noticeable. He splashed cold water over his face loosening the stiff skin. He stretched his face, making different expressions. Skin pulled under his hair follicles.

A quiet atmosphere in the kitchen found his dad engulfed in the morning paper. An outburst showed his father's upset. "What a shame! A person's home isn't safe anymore."

Brock spun around with his glass of orange juice in hand. He imagined holding the cold glass to his head for comfort. "What do you mean Dad?"

"One of our neighbors was terrorized last night. A couple of juveniles were out having some fun. The only problem is that the man took a minor heart attack from all the excitement. He is hospitalized for a couple of days."

Brock choked on his juice. He cleared his throat of thick orange pulp. "Which neighbor?"

Dad looked up at him. "Mr. Challens from 128 Sandy Road. What happened to your face, son? Your eyes are puffy."

"Nothing." Brock turned his head. The throbbing escalated from outrageous guilt. Mr. Challens was in critical care because he took matters into his own hands. The police had reason to charge him for something now. Brock snapped back to the present. "I guess I didn't get enough sleep last night."

He set his glass down and picked up the paper. Brock skimmed the article. His stomach ran a marathon in seconds. Justin popped into his mind. Sickness switched to anger. "Maybe I should stay home today Dad. I am pretty exhausted."

Dad frowned. "You've missed quite a bit of time the last couple of weeks. Are you sure there isn't anything wrong?"

Brock bit his lower lip, concealing the cut and pain at that moment. "Everything is fine."

"You can't be over worked?" Dad grinned.

He glued himself to the printed page. Eye contact was a mistake when Brock lied. "I probably need to go to bed earlier at night. I'll be at work tomorrow for sure."

After his dad left he called Justin. An answering machine picked up. Brock left an urgent message. No word from the leader after an hour. Restlessness grew into anxiety. Reality sunk in and presented a new picture. Brock feared his leader had turned him into the police. Justin threatened to get even with him and maybe this was his revenge.

Creative work relaxed Brock so he finished working on a birdhouse. Hours passed with no call from Justin. He worried about the old man but didn't know what to do. Noon came and Brock decided it was better to think on a full stomach. He planned his next step of action.

The doorbell startled him. He raced for the entrance but stopped. Was it the police, he thought? He peeked through the living room blinds. The front step was hidden from view. He peered through a tiny peephole in the door and nobody was there. A heavy sigh released. It had to be a salesperson or somebody with the wrong address.

The doorbell frightened him a second time. Someone waited

outside. He had to answer the door. His heart skipped beat when the door opened.

9

JUDGMENT DAY

Dressed in his favourite jeans with ripped knees and a black T-shirt, Justin stepped inside.

"Hey, Statler. What's the emergency?"

"Haven't you read the morning paper?"

Justin shrugged.

Brock was nervous. "Mr. Challens had a heart attack last night. He's under observation for a few days. This time you went too far."

The tall boy strutted around the entrance forcing his broad shoulders back. A devious smile appeared. "So I got him good. He knows who the boss is now." Justin gestured to his chest. "Who got the last laugh, Statler?"

Blood pressure rose. Agitation changed to anger and Brock's face burned. He kicked his toe against the entrance wall, realizing it hurt. His leader's grin made his blood boil. "Listen to me! If he takes another attack or dies, you're in serious trouble. We both are. Forget about your stupid revenge for a minute. Can you handle someone's death on your conscience?"

Justin jabbed his puppet in the chest. "I'm not the stupid one here and don't yell at me, Statler."

Arms tensed as Brock clenched his fists. He grabbed the ringleader's arm, squeezing with all his force. "If you're so smart, don't you think you should see if the man is all right? I think you owe him that much courtesy."

Justin yanked his puppet's hands free. He shoved Brock against the wall, staring down at him. "I don't care how the old guy is. Where do you get off telling me what to do and what to think?"

A state of confusion took over. Brock performed an unconscious act, not thinking what consequences were in store. He assumed control by reverse psychology. "Don't you want to make sure you did a good job? Maybe he'll go to a nursing home and all your problems will be solved."

The idea triggered a response. Justin let go. He snubbed his nose, prancing around the hall.

"Let's make sure the troublemaker won't cause any more problems."

The main entrance was empty at North Central Hospital. A sign posted visiting hours from two p.m. to four p.m. It was always quiet before visiting began. Brock glanced at the clock. They had fifteen minutes to check on Mr. Challens before activity started.

Brock followed Justin to the front desk. He smiled at people coming and going through the automated doors. Hospitals had a funny smell, a nauseous smell. He hated the stuffiness like all air conditioning was shut off or something. Hospitals never seemed to have fresh air circulating.

A stern looking woman sat at her computer. "May I help you boys?"

Justin thumped his hands onto the counter, drumming

against the wood. "Where can we find Mr. Challens?"

The receptionist typed in some data. "When was he brought in?"

"Last night," said Justin.

The woman tapped the keyboard. "Fourth floor, but you will have to ask for the room at the nurse's station."

Relieved to find an empty elevator, Brock stepped inside. He refrained from being recognized. The elevator's quick movement dropped Brock's lower body to the floor. He lost his stomach! He grabbed the black bar running along the wall of the square enclosure. The elevator jolted, opening doors onto fourth floor. He stepped weightless onto the tiled floor. Brock stood still while his body kept moving.

The narrow corridor stretched both ways. Vomit smothered the hall. A nurse rushed down to a room across from the elevator. The nurse's station stood on the opposite side of large swinging doors.

"That's where we go." Brock pointed.

Justin pushed through the heavy doors, leading to the nurse's station. The doors swung shut behind Brock. Stale air consumed his nostrils. The increased temperature suffocated him. A wipe of the forehead removed sweat droplets. A wide 'L' shaped desk sat to the left where a cheerful nurse greeted them.

"Which room is Mr. Challens in?" Justin asked.

The young nurse observed the visitors. Her smile faded. "May I ask who is inquiring?"

Brock leaned forward with a quick reply, "We are his grandsons. Our parents told us what those terrible boys did to him last night and we came to see how he was doing."

A strange odor lingered from the room across the hall. Brock plugged his nose. It smelled like rubbing alcohol that his mother used to put on cuts to stop bleeding.

The nurse resumed her tender manner. "We have to be careful with visitors, especially when patients are involved with the police. Our patient's safety comes first."

A metal tray on legs sat beside the desk. It had rollers on the legs for easy movement. Tiny paper cups placed in rows lined the top of the tray. Some had one or two pills and others had a stack of colored tablets in them.

The nurse checked her chart as she played with the stethoscope wrapped around her neck.

"The first room on your left. Don't be long boys. Your grandfather needs his rest."

Brock waved.

"Tell your grandfather I'll be in soon," the nurse added.

Lying was not in nature to Brock but somehow became redundant. Guilt stabbed him as he convinced himself that small white lies meant the safety of Mr. Challens. Honesty played no part at this time.

Justin strolled down the hall, swinging his arms. He marched into the room.

Brock hated hospitals, since his grandfather passed away. North Central Hospital was his least favourite place to visit. Nausea set in as he neared the old man's room. The weight of his head tightened for a spin off. A fainting spell came on whenever he was nauseous. He remembered Grandpa lying in bed. A chill raced up his arms producing a quiver. He licked dry lips and walked down the hall. A steady step ensured his balance. Maintenance personnel mopped square tiles ahead of him. The cleaners stung his eyes making them water. He approached room 405. Brock grabbed the middle of his stomach and stopped. A deep voice spoke behind him. Brock swung around and froze. Two uniformed men carried on a serious conversation with the nurse. The woman pointed towards him. His last meal rose. A whiff of antiseptic increased the rising food in his stomach. No exits available when you need them, thought Brock.

The police officers strolled in his direction. "What are you doing here young man?" asked an older officer.

Brock glanced at the hospital room. "I came to see Mr. Challens." Wet hands secured his abdomen. He was afraid to move.

"Are you family?"

"A friend." Brock lowered his head and waited for a third degree. He paid attention to rapid convulsions taking place inside his stomach.

The younger officer went inside the room. Justin slipped past the police officer, running into the second officer. He was apprehended outside the door. "Easy son. What's your hurry?"

Confusion crossed the ringleader's face. "I was leaving." Justin pulled his arm but couldn't get free.

Brock wondered how he got into this mess. The officer led Justin into the room and the other officer beckoned him to join them.

The door offered security and that's where Brock remained. The old man nestled in his bed. He looked like Grandpa wrapped in the white sheet and light blanket. He wasn't safe even in the hospital, thought Brock.

Justin pulled from the officer, but the grip tightened. "Don't try anything. Now why are you here?"

"I all ready told you."

"How about telling me again," asked the officer.

"I was leaving."

"Is this gentleman a friend of yours?" The policeman pointed to the bed.

Justin shifted, giving a yank for freedom. He failed the second time.

"Why would the nurse say you were this man's grandson?"

"I don't know. Why don't you ask her? She's the one who said we were," snapped Justin.

The private washroom door swung open. Brock grabbed the door handle beside him. A middle-aged woman stepped into the room, her chestnut hair tucked in place on the back of her head. A white, nurse's uniform hung from the slender frame.

Color faded from the leader's round face. The nurse paused. She looked at Justin and then the police officers. "What are you doing here? What's going on?"

The nurse made the leader nervous. She seemed surprised to see Justin. Brock had no idea where this episode led. Fright braced him tighter against the wall for support.

Justin's voice cracked. "Mom! I was looking for you."

"Is something wrong?" asked Mrs. Galley.

"These two boys schemed up a story to get past the nurse's station. They presented themselves as Mr. Challens grandsons," said the officer.

Mrs. Galley pointed her finger at her son. "Did you do that, Justin?"

"They got everything mixed up, Mom. I was looking for you so I could get some money."

"There's been a terrible mistake, officer. Is there any harm in visiting a parent at work?"

The officer peered down at Justin, keeping a firm grip. "There is no harm, ma'am, unless Justin had other reasons for being in this room. We were informed that he was leaving, but now says he was looking for you, ma'am. The other boy confessed to visiting their friend."

"Justin, tell the officers why you are here?"

Brock's hand slipped off the handle. Sweaty palms wiped across his shirt. He looked at the man resting in bed. His grandfather's face appeared on the old man. The room became lopsided and his head lightened. Objects wavered in their place. All of the adults floated before him. He squinted to focus on the strangers around him.

Justin glanced at his puppet. Brock held himself together and regained his vision. The room stopped spinning. The verdict was in. A cold perspire turned Brock's skin clammy. The room twirled in slow motion as he slipped to the floor without feeling. Stars shot out through a dark blanket. Voices sounded in his head when he forced his eyes open.

"Are you okay?"

The slim figure knelt beside Brock, offering him a paper cup. "Drink this. You will feel better," said Mrs. Galley.

Weakened by his fainting spell, Brock took the drink of water in his shaking hands. The heat wave lifted with the onset of a chill. He wiped his face with the bottom of his shirt. A slow stance regenerated his balance to stand. A powerful odor seeped in from the hall. Hospital cleansers cleared his head in seconds.

"Thank you, Mrs. Galley."

"Heat does funny things to people. You'll be fine." She looked back at her son and continued, "Now Justin, why are you here?"

"You forgot to leave me money this morning so I came to find you."

Mrs. Galley had a pleasant smile. She reminded Brock of his mother's pretty features. He glanced at the bed noticing Mr. Challens had his own face again. His thoughts brought back memories of his grandfather's last day. He shook his head and waited for a confession from the ringleader.

"We can settle this officer." The nurse pulled a five-dollar bill from her uniform pocket and handed it to her son. "Don't spend it all at once. I didn't leave money today because I gave you some yesterday."

The police officer frowned. "It isn't that simple. We have different versions of a story here and nobody goes anywhere until we get the truth."

"I came for some money."

The officer looked at Brock. "What is your story, son?"

Brock melted on the spot. He was speechless. His leader's expression cautioned his reply. Honesty was his only chance. "I came to see my friend, Mr. Challens."

The young officer rubbed his short beard and observed Brock. He stepped into the conversation. "Seems we have two stories and the nurse swears that you boys insisted you were this man's grandsons. The only way to settle this is by asking you, ma'am. Is this man your son's grandfather?"

Mrs. Galley flushed. A red complexion set off her hazel eyes. She played with the wedding ring on her finger. The officer repeated the question.

A raspy voice startled everyone. "What is he doing here?"

Justin jumped away from the police officer. Brock backed into the wall, banging his arm on the door. Clumsiness was a nervous reaction for the Statler family.

Mrs. Galley reached for her patient, patting his hand. "It's okay Mr. Challens. No need for worry."

The man pulled himself up in bed, pointing at the leader. "Justin Galley, you destroyed my house. Let me get my hands on you."

The nurse held the man down. She reassured him, "You know Justin. My son didn't do this to you."

"I know him too well and yes, he is to blame for all of this mess." The old man struggled to get up. "I had a good look at him last night. I warned you to stay off my property and you won't listen." Mr. Challens grabbed at Justin.

Mrs. Galley caught the man's arm. "Lie back and rest. This excitement is not good for you."

Brock huddled in the corner with an eye on the open washroom door. He was too weak to run and frightened to death to speak.

The old man was wound up. Justin dashed between the officers, knocking Brock off balance.

The man sprung forward shaking his fist in the air. "You aren't getting away with it this time. I'm pressing charges and the courts will take care of you."

Justin sailed out the door and down the hall followed by the two uniforms.

Mrs. Galley conducted her bedside manners by tucking in sheets and trying to calm the man down. She tried relaxing him.

"Leave me alone." The man flung an arm at the nurse.

Brock peeked into the hall. Two uniforms headed back to the room with the tall figure. Stepping inside the door, he wondered what was next on the agenda. Justin kicked and pulled at his bodyguards as they entered the room.

"I wasn't near your place. You're a senile old man."

"Justin!" Mrs. Galley covered her mouth in shock.

"I've warned you many times that I was calling the police and nothing gets through to you."

"Without an eyewitness, you can't prove it was me. I don't see anyone coming forward to testify." Justin looked around the crowded room.

"I saw you." Mr. Challens turned to the police. "That's him. He is the one who destroyed my place last night."

The younger officer moved beside the bed. "Are you

positive this is the boy?"

"That's him." The old man pointed at the ringleader.

"There's been a mistake. You know my son isn't capable of such a terrible thing," interrupted Mrs. Galley.

The older officer focused on the tall boy. "Justin Galley! I remember paying a visit to your house last week. Were you not warned to leave this man alone? I also recall informing you that charges would result next time you did something."

Arms swung from his sides as Justin shouted, "I didn't do anything. The old man is losing it. I wasn't near his place. Right, Brock?"

Everyone faced the door. Four adults waited for a reply, but Brock remained silent. He wasn't able to talk, even if he knew the proper answer. His leader placed him in another awkward position. A sick man depended on him and this was no time to lie.

The young nurse's appearance broke the silence. "Is there a problem with your grandsons being here?"

"They aren't my grandsons," shouted Mr. Challens.

The officers waved the confused nurse out of the room. She left without a word.

Mrs. Galley lowered her head, holding her hands together. She looked as if she was praying. Brock knew it was too late for prayers.

Justin tapped his foot on the linoleum flooring. He presented his usual tough outer shell. Nothing frightened him, or at least didn't seem to.

"I'm going to ask you one more time. Why did you come to the hospital, Justin?"

The leader tossed his long hair and smirked at his puppet. Silence filled the enclosed room. Brock crept forward. He concentrated on a loose thread coming apart at the bottom of his shirt. He raised his head to a mean stare. Justin's look revealed a warning. The old man shook his head and Brock took the hint.

The policeman turned to Brock. "Do you have anything to say?"

Mr. Challens interrupted, "No need to bother the boy. Justin is the one you want. I want him charged with trespassing and vandalism."

"Mrs. Galley, will you come with us to police headquarters. We have no choice but to take your son in for suspicion of vandalizing private property, trespassing, and terrorizing a senior. We will need a statement from both of you and then take it from there."

The older officer took the leader's arm and read his rights. "Justin Galley, you are placed under arrest for trespassing, vandalism…"

Brock listened and watched all the commotion in a daze. He felt as though he was living someone else's nightmare. He wondered why Mr. Challens stopped him from speaking. The young officer approached Brock. "Will you come with us, son? We have a few questions to ask you."

He nodded. Brock wobbled behind the officer. His queasy stomach tightened and stretched the lining of his abdomen. He never dealt with police before. Two bodyguards escorted the gang leader down the hall. Brock followed the group past the nurse's station. He blushed when the young nurse winked at him. He was ashamed to be involved in the situation and terrified at what was next on the list. White walls closed in on both sides, the elevator suffocated him more, and the open entrance of the hospital was no comfort.

One officer put Justin into the police cruiser accompanied by his mother. The second policeman remained inside the lobby for questioning. The bright atmosphere gave no consolation to the darkness building inside. Brock took a seat on the firm red leather padding and waited for the line of fire. His rib cage crushed against his muscles feeling his middle section collapse with pressure.

"Brock, were you with Justin last night?"

"Yes."

"Was Justin at Mr. Challens house last night? If yes, did he damage this man's property and terrorize him?"

Brock released a deep sigh. The tall man looked down at him with authority. The police officer's compassionate manner made it easier to tell the truth. He nodded.

"I need a verbal answer, Brock."

"Yes, he was there and did all the damage. I was there too."

"What part did you play?"

Brock squeezed wet hands into a ball. The officer scribbled in his notepad. "I was a watchman. I yelled at Justin to stop and the man heard me. That's when he fell inside the house."

The young officer stuck the notepad into his pocket and held out his hand. "Thank you for your cooperation Brock. We may have to speak with you again. I need a phone number to contact your father. He needs to be informed about what's happened."

"Not my Dad."

"It's procedure. Your father has to be aware of the circumstances."

Brock gave his dad's work number. His dad was done work soon and would know all about his participation last night. The day turned out terrible and reached a climax. The tough part was witnessing his leader drive away in a police cruiser. It terrified him to think he could have been sitting next to Justin at that moment. His leader had problems and was a dysfunctional kid but pity escaped from Brock. He felt sorry the summer had to end this way for Justin. He wished the guy had listened to him.

Brock headed home reviewing the last few hours over and over again. His stomach settled but tension increased as he reached his driveway.

Brock sat at the kitchen table ripping up paper. Another torn piece fell into his pile. Explaining his actions to his father wasn't an easy task. Time ran out for organizing his thoughts. Dad's truck motored into the driveway. Brock's heart dropped and a lump formed in the middle of his neck when his dad entered the kitchen.

"Feeling better, son?"

"Kind of."

Mr. Statler put on a fresh pot of coffee. He joined his son, noticing the tiny pieces of paper. Fingers tapped against the wooden tabletop. "Police called me at work."

Brock sank into his chair. A shaky heartbeat kicked into overdrive. He was not ready for those words. Eye contact was limited. Guilt was too strong at this point for him to face his father.

"Your friend was picked up for terrorizing Mr. Challens. Police questioned your friendship with Justin. He gave an alibi for the two of you."

Brock lifted his head. "What alibi?"

"Supposedly, you and him were working on his go-cart last night. I wasn't much help, of course, because you never mentioned where you were going." Dad hesitated. "The police informed me that you were at the crime scene but you weren't involved as an offender. Is that true?"

His father's watchful eye agitated Brock. His body trembled knowing he had disappointed his dad. "Yes, I was there."

"This is serious, Brock. It's time you tell me what has been going on."

Guilt overwhelmed Brock on many counts but last night he was innocent. His unsteady speech began shaky, "I was there to protect the man." Brock felt sick but his emotions pushed outward. Tears swelled up his eyes.

His father raised his voice. "What happened? Why would you get involved in such a terrible incident?"

Brock rubbed away the waterworks exploding in his eyes. He shifted in his chair. An uncomfortable feeling settled because he hurt his father by dishonest actions. No explanation justified his behavior. It was truth time.

"Justin paid the man back for calling the police on him. He wanted to get even. I didn't know what he planned so I went to make sure nothing happened to the man."

Mr. Statler paced the floor. Brock felt his father's stern look. "Look at me, son."

Fright filled his dad's eyes among the anger and hurt. "Why didn't you tell me, or someone else, what was happening? Did you think you were capable of handling this kind of situation alone?"

Brock sniffled. "It would have been worse if I didn't yell. Justin swung a shovel at the man."

Dad shook his head. "It all sounds like a horror movie. I missed some facts somewhere along the way. How about putting the pieces together for me?"

"You wouldn't believe it Dad? I'm not sure if I know what's been happening."

His father crossed his arms, taking a deep breath. "At this point, nothing would surprise me. We have all night so tell me what caused this incident."

Brock shuddered at consequences for telling the truth. He organized past events in his mind. He wondered how much his dad knew. He confessed, "Everyone has left me and I felt like no one cared about me anymore. It's like I was abandoned. I thought if I changed into someone who fit in with other kids then I wouldn't need to be alone. I would have something to do this summer. I thought if I stood up to people and took risks like the kids at school do then I could have more friends to hang out with during the holidays."

"What do you mean everyone has left you?"

"Mom left, Grandpa died, and Trenton left. I didn't have anyone left to spend time with for the summer. I thought if I worked at Wilson's Garage this summer I could spend more time with you." Brock choked up watching his father's blushing face and glassy eyes ready to burst.

"What happened between your mother and I has nothing to do with you. Don't ever feel guilty for our mistakes. Our divorce was a mutual decision. You never did anything wrong Brock. Your grandpa's time had come and we don't have any control over matters concerning death. As for Trenton, well he will be back after his visit." Dad paused before he continued, "Son, my job keeps me pretty busy and sometimes emergencies call for weekend work. We have to compromise to make things work and between the both of us we can arrange more time together. You should never feel alone. We have each other to look out for one another."

His father grabbed him with the tightest hug ever. "We will continue this conversation later. What I'd like to know is why you befriended Justin?"

"Justin liked go-carts, he was carefree and always seemed to have things to occupy his time so I jumped at the prospects. I joined his gang and we hung out together. He told me problems he had with his stepfather and he hated Mr. Challens for causing trouble."

His father interrupted, "Why do you think Mr. Galley is

Justin's stepfather?"

"Justin said he was his step-father. He told me whenever the police showed up his stepfather abused him. I wanted to stop him from bothering the old man so the police wouldn't be involved but he got angrier. I told him to work things out with his father but he wouldn't listen."

"Mr. Galley is Justin's real father, not stepfather. What makes you think his father abused him?"

The question stunned Brock. "He had a terrible black shiner. His eye was swollen and that awful scar is from his father."

"Justin told you all of this?"

"Yes. He blamed the old man for his problems with his dad and planned to scare the guy but he went crazy. Justin took a shovel after Mr. Challens and that's when I yelled for him to stop. I tried to save the man. I didn't break the law." Brock sobbed into his hands.

His father remained quiet as he filled his coffee mug. The silence in the room and his father's sad expression made Brock feel worse.

He remembered Grandpa saying, *"It is good having a clear conscience and the only way to do that is getting things off your chest."*

Watching his father doubted Brock's previous advice. Honesty caused pain and suffering for him and his dad all because of his immature actions.

Dad sipped his coffee. Wrinkled lines tightened up his blue eyes. Black hair turned gray by the minute. His gentle voice continued their conversation, "Brock do you know anything else about Justin's background?"

Brock switched positions on the hard seat. "No, why would you ask a weird question like that?"

His father's caring words grabbed his attention. "Justin is a very emotional kid and has been in trouble many times."

Interest sprouted antennas. "He lied to me about his dad and…"

His father interrupted, "Son, he lied to you about everything. Justin is a troubled boy in desperate need of counseling. His parents have done everything to keep him out of trouble. Maybe juvenile authorities will be able to help since he has been charged with an offence."

Brock jumped from his seat. He paced the square tiles, shaking his head. He slapped his head, realizing it was too late. "I knew something was wrong. I couldn't talk sense to him at all. Why didn't you tell me this before?"

"The sergeant filled me in today when he called."

"Justin was never charged before?"

"That's right, son. Police suspected him numerous times and somehow he managed to keep off the offenders list."

Brock stood beside his father. He worried over the next answer but had to ask. "What happens to Justin and I now?"

Dad wrapped his arm around Brock. "Justin appears in juvenile hearing tomorrow morning. The police will inform us about the outcome."

"And what about me!"

"First of all, you are not charged for anything and you won't get your day in court. Mr. Challens requested that he handle your sentencing. You will receive your verdict tomorrow at nine o'clock."

Surprised by the outcome Brock hugged his dad. His grip loosened and he frowned.

"Tomorrow morning at nine."

"Yes. That is when Mr. Challens will give you all the details of your sentencing."

His shoulders dropped fifty pounds. Closure to a crucial

period ended, bringing the onset of a new experience and even larger challenge than he could ever imagine.

"Dad, I know I deserve whatever is handed to me because I am guilty. I feel more responsible than Justin, for what happened. I could have prevented all of this."

His father looked up at him. "You did what any twelve-year-old would have done. Trying to help a friend make wise choices when you know their actions are wrong is being a good friend. The only thing you are guilty of is not seeking adult advice."

"I guess I've learned a lifetime of lessons in the past month. At least I get jail time without the bars." Brock grinned. The heaviness disappeared with the worst part over. Mr. Challens seemed reasonable and Brock felt positive about any sentence handed down by the man.

"You might not be so spunky after meeting Mr. Challens. He's a perfect match for you and will probably teach more than you want to learn."

Brock turned at the kitchen doorway. "What's that supposed to mean?"

"You'll see tomorrow."

Maybe stiffer penalties existed for juveniles than Brock ever considered.

10

CONFINED FREEDOM

The neighborhood came to life on Sandy Road. Birds chirped from branches, and dogs barked the arrival of a beautiful Friday morning.

A small home exposed itself in the sunlight. Extensive damage horrified Brock. He stopped at the end of the narrow driveway filled with guilt. Escape crossed his mind with thoughts of confronting the victim.

Earth clumped in the empty flowerbeds. Cans, wrappers, leftovers, plastic bottles and containers smothered the green lawn. Two metal garbage cans lay upside down in the middle of the yard. Brock pinched his nose at rotting food baking in the sun. He inhaled through his mouth not to consume the stench. Uprooted cedar shrubs and rose bushes tangled in piles. Plants scattered the ground in a rainbow.

A tall man greeted Brock. His white hair sparkled in the morning light. He pointed at the yard. "A lot of anger expressed here."

Brock reviewed Wednesday night's performance. He was appalled at such destruction. He faced his consequences for unexplained participation. Humility kept him quiet. A slumped figure eased down the steps. The pale man dragged his body in short steps. His slender fingers rubbed over scratched bricks on the outer wall. "I'll have to consult someone about this."

Brock introduced himself. "I'm Brock Statler, sir." Apparent strength in the man's handshake surprised him.

"Glad to see you are punctual. That is important on a job. You may require a certificate for jack-of-all trades," Mr. Challens said.

"I can fix this mess, sir. The damaged bricks might be tough."

"Honest and punctual, a good combination. Shall we go inside and talk business?" The man extended his hand towards the house and Brock followed.

Inside, a small kitchen displayed a round wooden table sitting in the far corner surrounded by two chairs. Newspapers covered the surface. The counter top sparkled clean. Two cups sat in a single sink, holding a handful of silverware.

The elderly man motioned to the table. "Have a seat and make room for two cups."

Mr. Challens took his time preparing drinks. He carried coffee and chocolate milk to the table. "This will get us started." He smiled.

Brock sipped his cold milk. Curiosity ended the waiting. "Sir, why didn't the police charge me?"

The old man rested his arms on the table. "Saving a person's life is not a crime. You took no part in vandalizing my property, did you?"

"No, sir."

"Why should you be punished for a crime you never committed?"

"I watched Justin do everything. I could have prevented all

this damage but I didn't."

The man stirred sugar into his coffee. He spoke casual. "Why didn't you prevent it, Brock?"

"Justin was going to report me to the police as their suspect."

Mr. Challens passed a plate of mixed cookies to Brock. "Sounds like Justin Galley played two victims at the same time. The boy uses people to his advantage."

Brock's interest perked. "Why are you sentencing me if I'm not guilty of anything?"

"I never pressed charges against you because you are as much a victim as I am. Punishment is for offenders and you don't fit that category. Constructive guidance is what you need."

"What is constructive guidance?"

The old man smiled. "I do my homework before hiring a stranger to work around my home. Let's say I am updated on Brock Statler. Why don't you explain to me what constructive guidance is after you've served your time."

Confusion surrounded his sentence and this *'constructive guidance'* made Brock curious.

"Have you known Justin for a long time?"

Mr. Challens frowned. Focused on his cup of coffee he lifted his head. "Son, let me tell you something about Justin. Mrs. Galley was one of my students twenty odd years ago and kept in touch. Two years ago, problems escalated with Justin and she asked for my help."

"What problems? What help?"

The old man continued, "Justin was a rebellious young lad when the Galleys moved to Northshore. His studies fell and his mother asked me to tutor him. Of course, the boy hated school and refused my help. He blamed me because he had classes after school."

"Is that why he was so mad at you?"

"Justin hates authority. He rebelled when he had to learn. He took his anger out on me because I was the teacher." Mr. Challens sipped his coffee. "What brought the two of you boys together?"

Brock lowered his head, ashamed of his circumstances. "My best friend went away for the summer and I was bored. Justin asked to hang out and work on his go-cart with him. I was excited because I found someone besides Trenton who shared my interest."

"The boy does have talent but applies it the wrong way. What other interests do you have Brock?"

"I work at Wilson's Auto Garage, or I did until now. I want to be a mechanic like my dad. I took over my grandfather's business building birdhouses and feeders. My dad and I are saving for a new computer so I can use for high school studies. It's supposed to improve my reading and writing skills. I'm in Special Education class with Miss Johnson. I have Non-Verbal Learning Disability. My reading isn't very good and I have problems spelling."

"Yes, Non-Verbal or known as Perceptual Learning Disability. I'm quite familiar with your disability. Students can be reluctant about reading when it is difficult learning. Do you have social problems because of your special classes?"

Brock scratched his head. "I'm not popular at school because everyone calls me stupid. Trenton is my only friend and when he left for holidays I had nobody. I thought everyone abandoned me and didn't care about me anymore so I decided to change into a different person."

"What made you think you were abandoned and needed to change?"

"My parents are divorced, my grandpa died this spring, and

Trenton went away for two months. I was lonely. I thought if I became more daring and stood up for myself, I could belong to a group and experience adventure. When Justin showed up, I thought my summer had changed. He was complete opposite of me and always teased me at school. He was the one person who could challenge me the most and he did, but not for the better."

"You have learned a great deal so far this summer, haven't you Brock?"

"Yes, sir."

"Trenton is your friend and you've seen how Justin's type of a friend behaves. You have to believe in yourself first. A person can't pretend to be someone else. Did you like who you were before, Brock?"

"I guess so. At least I never got into any trouble, not serious stuff."

"I must say you sure are ambitious." Mr. Challens winked. "Your ambitious nature will be put to the test this month."

"The whole month."

The old man emptied cold coffee into the sink. "That's right. You're stuck with me for the month of August. Let's take a look at the damage and organize a schedule."

The back yard was worse than the rest of the property. Brock felt terrible. Justin damaged everything in sight.

The old man handed Brock a pen and pad from his pocket. "Make a list of repairs. We'll go through them so nothing is overlooked."

Brock wrote out his list. Damaged birdbath, three birdhouses, flowerbeds and pots, garden hose, and chips taken out of the back shed. The extensive damage led to the front yard. Labor involved fixing flowerbeds, picking up garbage, glass, and broken flowerpots. The scratched concrete was a professional job. Hours included replanting shrubs, fixing dented garbage cans, and a broken sprinkler.

"Does that cover everything young man?"

"I guess so." Brock sighed, "It looks like you need a handyman."

Mr. Challens smiled. "Make a list of a few items to do each day. Between the two of us, we can figure out how to repair these things. I have other duties to mix into your schedule."

"What duties? I thought I was here to clean up Justin's mess."

The man pointed around the yard. "After all this is cleaned up I want you to plant flowers, fill in holes, and plant grass seed. You will have weeding, mowing grass, trimming, and watering every week, besides indoor work, and errands to run."

A detailed schedule tired him out. His jail had no bars but the sentence was hard labor.

"Don't be discouraged, son. There's a lot of work to do. Take it step by step and time will pass quick."

The man sounded like his grandfather. It made sense not worrying over all the work he faced. Detailed instructions simplified job demands.

"A change of scenery is needed for the neighbors so you better start in the front. Pick up all the garbage, bag the rooted shrubs and plants, and clean up the glass in the driveway. When you're finished hose down the drive and come see me," instructed the old man.

Brock found green garbage bags in the back shed. He picked up larger items by hand and used a fan rake for food and smaller items. The noon sun felt like a hundred degrees. Beads of sweat beckoned for a rest. Propped against the lawn rake Brock examined his remaining work.

Twisted shrubs and plants were dumped into the metal can. He dragged the container along his way. The green carpet looked neater with the odd pothole peeking out of the ground. Brock found black electrical tape in the shed. He bandaged the long green snake, connecting the hose to the waterspout. A wide broom pushed glass into piles along the paved driveway. He picked up the glass and hosed down remaining dirt.

A rough voice called, "Lunch break."

Brock washed off the dirt in the kitchen sink. Cold water refreshed him after hard work. A small hand towel hung from the cupboard door. His growling stomach announced hunger. He peeked around to see what was for lunch. The table and counter were bare.

Mr. Challens opened the refrigerator door and pointed on the top shelf. "There is leftover pork and sliced bologna. The bread and butter are in the cupboard. Knives are in that drawer. Fix us a sandwich and we'll continue our talk."

The man sat without another word. Shocked and feeling awkward snooping around in someone else's kitchen Brock prepared lunch. He slapped ingredients together for pork sandwiches with mustard. A fast stroke divided the bread. He carried two small plates with his gourmet lunch. Brock fumbled the plates setting them down on the table.

Mr. Challens picked up a sandwich and bit into it. "No need to be shy boy. Eat up."

Brock nibbled at the whole wheat bread. He disliked bologna and wasn't crazy about pork. He finished a quiet meal and cleaned up the dishes.

"Sit down for a minute, son."

Brock took a seat. Worried lines stretched over the man's face. "Is something wrong?"

"Police headquarters called with Justin's verdict."

Brock leaned closer. The news wasn't good, he thought.

"Justin was placed in detention center this morning for two

weeks. He is ordered to one year probation and thirty hours of community work." The man fell quiet.

Brock twiddled his thumbs. He scrunched his shoulders. "I thought they would keep him in detention longer. What happens after he gets out?"

"This is his first offence and he shouldn't be in detention. The judge decided discipline was needed and confined to security premises would benefit Justin. He has weekly appointments with a probation officer upon his release. Probation will be extended if he misses a session or breaks the law."

Brock lowered his head. The zipper appeared before him casting an angry stare. The thought became frightening. Justin's last words haunted him and a nail-biting contest broke out. His leader promised to come back for him and nothing stopped Justin's revenge.

"Are you afraid of Justin?"

Brock avoided eye contact. He resumed in a quiet nature. "He has a good reason to get me now. I wasn't charged for anything and that will make him mad."

"Let's take it one day at a time and see what happens. There isn't anything to worry about at present. We have two weeks before our visitor arrives."

"You sound positive he'll return for payback. You think he'll try something else after being locked up in a detention center?"

Mr. Challens poured himself another cup of tea. His face relayed Brock's own thoughts.

"You spent the past month with Justin. Don't you think he'll try again?"

"Justin never gives up. He will have a master plan ready. It could be the most evil of all." Brock lost his appetite and pushed his sandwich aside. "Do you think Justin's father will beat him when he gets out?"

The old man screwed up his face and slipped back into his chair. "Why would you think his father would abuse him, Brock?"

"His father gave him that terrible scar and a few black eyes. I know because I saw the shiners."

"Brock, there is no truth to that story. Justin did those things to himself, not his father or anyone else."

Nothing made sense to Brock. "How did he get that scar?"

"Justin takes temper tantrums which are severe compared to normal fits of rage. He threw himself against the corner of a counter during one of his worst episodes. It is like a person having a convulsion and not knowing what is happening to them at the time. Justin never remembers what he has done and blames his father. He believes his father is out to get him because of his strict discipline methods."

"Is that why he makes up stories about his father?"

"Yes. Justin craves attention from people who don't know his circumstances. That way he gets sympathy and his own way. Bossing people around is a way of being in control and he enjoys having the upper hand."

"I figured he was a mixed up kid but never thought Justin was so disturbed. He really did a number on me the past month."

"You can't judge a book by its cover, Brock. What seems easy to read on the outside may be complicated inside."

The man was right about Justin. The more Brock new about his ringleader the deeper confusion grew. Mr. Challens broke his concentration. He handed him a piece of paper with a schedule for the week. He expressed his thoughts with a twisted expression.

"Read what I have prepared and make sure you understand what has to be done."

Brock raced over the words on the page.

"I mean out loud. I want you to be clear about your duties and ask questions before you start the jobs."

Brock stalled. Words scrambled together complicating his reading abilities. The first sentence stumped him. *"Monday morning in...veent..."*

"In-ven-tree." Mr. Challens leaned over Brock's shoulder and pointed to each word as he read the list. "I'll go over the jobs again when you come on Monday. That way we won't forget anything."

"What time do I start?"

"Can you come Monday to Friday from nine until five o'clock. The weekends are your time."

Brock nodded.

The man looked at his watch. "It is getting late so I want you to tidy up the carport. Put all the garbage into one corner, roll up the hose, and straighten up the shovels, rakes and whatever else is lying around out there. Let me know when you are finished."

Brock went outside as directed. He tidied up the carport and completed his jobs. He double-checked the yard for any supplies he missed. He picked up broken pieces of the birdhouses and examined them. Mr. Challens startled him from the back door.

"Do you think there is anything to salvage?"

He conducted a thorough check. "I would replace the birdhouses with new ones. The wood is split and not much good."

"You are free to go, Brock. Do you have any questions?"

Brock walked over to the back step raising an awkward hand to the man. "Thank you for handling my sentencing. I'm sorry for what happened to you and your property. I will work hard and aim to correct my impulsive behavior in the future."

Mr. Challens' gentle handshake reassured him. "I should thank you, Brock. You put in some good hours today. Don't let bad judgment bother you, everyone makes mistakes."

"I will have your property back in shape before you know it." Brock spun around. "I hope you feel better soon."

"See you Monday morning, Brock."

"I can come on weekends, too."

"A visit would be nice." The man waved.

Brock rushed home energized. He unlocked the back door with his house key and hopped into the shower. The first day of sentencing washed down the drain. Comfortable jogging pants and an old T-shirt prepared him for work. He used valuable time to the minute.

Scrap plywood sat in the corner of his workshop. He chose appropriate materials for his feeder. Pre-cut pieces of wood saved time. One piece measured eight inches long and seven inches wide. It was perfect for the base. Three pieces of plywood cut seven inches by eight and three-quarter inches set aside for the sides and back. A new piece of wood marked an eight-by-eight-inch square cut for the roof. He put the roof aside to saw when his dad came home.

Brock placed the base of his feeder on the workbench. Wood glue joined two sides and a back. He sat the three-sided frame flesh with the corners of the base. The fit was close after sanding finished the touch ups. He ran glue along the bottom walls and stuck them to the base. His work pleased him.

Wood scraps produced narrow pieces for the opening section of the feeder. A seven-inch long piece glued to the front of the base. This prevented seed from spilling out. Two three-quarter inch blocks were cut. Attached to the front of the base, he connected the blocks to the longer piece. Brock glued the small parts together. They formed a slight ridge around the front opening. The birdhouse opening, sides and back sections were glued together. He heard his dad come home. "Down here, Dad."

His father paused at the doorway concentrating on Brock's legs. "No chains! You must have been good today." His father laughed and ruffled the top of his head.

Brock smoothed his short hair. "It wasn't that bad, Dad. Mr. Challens is totally the opposite from what I expected. It was okay. Anything would have been better than where Justin's spending time."

"Looks like the makings of a new house."

"Mr. Challens birdhouses were destroyed so I'm surprising him with a feeder to make him feel better. I waited for you to come home so I could saw the last piece."

Dad examined the project. "Impressive. What kind of feeder is this?"

"I call it my 'all purpose' feeder. It holds up to three pounds of seed. The roof protects the seed from getting wet in rain and it is good for different kinds of birds. It is great for Northshore because we have Chickadees, Nuthatches, Sparrows, and Finches."

"You've become quite the inventor, haven't you? Let me know when you strike it rich and I'll quit my job to work for you."

"I found blueprints Grandpa stashed away. He sold quite a few of these feeders."

"Go ahead and cut the wood, son. I'll fix dinner."

Brock cut out the roof. He found tiny hinges in a drawer of his caddy tray. He screwed the hinges onto the extended back and the roof. The lopsided roof managed to lift and close. It served the purpose of cleaning out the feeder. Dad's third call for dinner caught Brock's attention.

He rushed through dinner and escaped into the basement to check on the drying process. Brock examined all details of his creation.

The roof wasn't perfect but possessed all necessary requirements. A one-inch overhang provided water run off. The roof protected birdseed from other birds eating it. Brock searched for plastic. He had one sheet left somewhere. A piece looked like the perfect measurements for the front of the feeder. He applied glue to the plastic and realized it was short on one side. He had just enough room to spread a thin line of glue. Brock pressed the plastic against the opening. It fit close to the edges.

He admired the completed project with pride. His all-purpose feeder was the right height and width. A plastic sheet protected seeds from changing weather. Plastic covered the top down to a one-inch open space at the bottom. Room remained for pecking seeds and letting them fall onto the platform.

A quarter of an inch hole drilled in each corner of the floor was the final stage for drainage. This provided proper drains releasing any water from inside the feeder. A coat of beige water based exterior paint finished the feeder. Paint sealed the wood through year round weather conditions. A painted feeder lasted longer and was more useful. Brock was thrilled over his achievements. He sketched plans for a birdhouse he thought Mr. Challens would like.

His thoughts centered on the old man as he turned in for the night. He was fascinated by the knowledge his new friend possessed. Mr. Challens lived in seclusion according to neighbors but they didn't know the extent of his talent. The old man peaked Brock's curiosity. He was determined to discover secret talents hidden by the man.

11

THE STALKER

"Good morning, Mr. Challens."

Brock's friend enjoyed the morning sunshine from his lawn chair. He squinted against the sun.

"Aren't we chipper today? Bet you bought that new computer you'd been saving for."

"How did you guess?" The bounce in his step or stretched grin must have given a hint, thought Brock. He rode on a cloud. Humidity wasn't even a problem this morning. Flowers perfumed the air with a special scent. A pesky bee buzzed around his head without annoying him.

"The only thing that would put you in good spirits. The thought of school starting isn't exciting news for a boy your age, is it?"

"You're right. Besides being a gorgeous day, and seeing a clean yard for a change, I have a new computer. I'm anxious for school now so I can do assignments at home instead of staying late to finish them."

Mr. Challens sipped his coffee. The August air kept him comfortable along with his cardigan sweater. He wore the same kind Grandpa had with two big pockets and buttons down the front. Grandpa loved the outdoors in cool or hot weather and Mr. Challens was the same.

"I must be too easy on you, Brock. After two weeks you still show up punctual as ever."

"I'm ready to tackle anything, sir."

The aging man led way to the house. He moved free with a spring in his step. The old guy was spunky when he felt good.

Mr. Challens opened the door. "We'll start inside."

Brock sat in his usual spot at the round table. The man freshened up his coffee. "Do you want something to eat or drink?"

"No thank you."

The humped figure fumbled through papers on the tabletop. He looked around the kitchen unable to find what he searched for. He pointed to the hall. "Brock go into my study and get my note pad from the desk, will you."

Brock raised his hands in confusion. "Where is your study?"

"First door on your left."

Bookshelves lined one complete wall of the small room. Stacked boxes in a corner displayed books, manuscripts, and notes hanging over the edges. A large wooden desk sat under the window. A full-grown pine tree waved its branches outside. An organized desk occupied office gadgets placed in handy spots. A computer sat on one side of the mahogany desk and a printer rested on a short stand. The note pad centered between pens, a journal, and a calculator. Brock studied the hardbound journal. He wondered what the man wrote. He viewed the rest of the room upon leaving.

He handed the pad to Mr. Challens. "You have a real office in there. Have you read every book on those shelves?"

The man's face wrinkled with a sparkle in his brown eyes.

"Yes son, I have. It took many years but I read each one. Are you a reader?"

Brock shook his head. "I don't like reading but I'm supposed to. My special education teacher says it is good practice for my memory and strengthens my vocabulary. If I read lots it helps improve my spelling and writing."

The man pushed the notepad and a pen across to Brock. "Do you hate reading because you have to or because you haven't found an interesting book to read?"

"Both reasons I guess. How did you know? My school never has good books for our class to read. They only have stuff for grade two and three classes. Reading about kids my own age is more interesting."

The man responded with a nod. "There should be more choices for older students with learning problems. We didn't have much to choose from either when I was a kid. Sometimes I wonder why more of us didn't end up being slow readers."

Brock listened to the man's serious tone. The news shocked him. "You were a slow reader?"

"Yes I was."

"You are a retired teacher. How could you teach if you had trouble reading?"

"I worked hard and studied long hours. I have Perceptual Learning Disability the same as you do."

"How did you ever read all those books, go to teachers college, and learn everything?"

"Back in my day professionals had no idea disabilities existed. Through years of teaching I discovered so many students with the same problems. I learned how to cope with learning problems and pushed myself hard to be the best that I could. I taught regular classes in the beginning. I studied more about disabilities affecting children and decided teaching students with learning disabilities was my way of saying thank you for what I learned."

"Wow! Do you write in your journal every day to keep as a memoir?"

"Every day since I was a boy. When you live far from your neighbors and have nobody to chum with, writing is your best friend. Now, take that pad and write your duties for today. Do them in any order but have them finished by the end of the day."

Brock grinned as he wrote his job list. His grandfather sat with him at the table. Mr. Challens spoke stern but was a kind person. His grandfather was strict, full of rules, and understanding in his way.

"What's so funny, Brock?"

"Nothing!" He chuckled. "You remind me of someone that's all."

"I hope that is a compliment." The man smiled.

Brock continued reviewing a busy day of chores. Work became easier the past two weeks since he completed most of the hard labor. He finished filling in holes on the lawn, leveled flowerbeds, and raked broken branches.

His chores included planting flowers, shrubs, and rose bushes. He circled birdhouses on the paper because he waited for the perfect time to give his gift. Birdbath repairs waited until later that week. He finished his list and gardening was top priority.

"Done."

"Will you read today's front page headlines in the paper?" Mr. Challens pointed.

Brock looked over the headlines and chose the easiest ones. Challenged by the next headline on the page, he hesitated.

"Take your time and sound out the words by syllables. It makes reading natural that way."

Brock sounded each word. *"Re-seye-dents of North-shore. Residents of Northshore are safe again."* He smiled and proceeded with the article. The man never interrupted. Brock corrected himself through the entire piece.

"Very well done. Great improvement, Brock! You'll be a fluent reader in no time."

"Thanks. I get nervous and make mistakes when I read to someone. I find it easy reading to you because you don't correct me whenever I mess up." Brock's accomplishment proved his ability to spot his own errors and act in a positive manner. He felt relaxed and confident in front of his new friend instead of ashamed.

"Practice makes perfect. Now let's start work and I'll call you at lunch." The man winked.

Brock carried flats of colorful flowers to the front yard. His nose twitched with the different aromas. He arranged taller plants near the house and worked his way to the edging. He transplanted dahlias, snapdragons, and pansies into pre-dug holes. Waxed begonias were his favourite. The smooth coated texture reminded him of planting red and pink begonias every year with his mother. Brock surrounded the edge of the flowerbed with tiny begonias. He leveled the black soil neatly. He tore open a bag of white pebbles and spread them over the soil. The tiny stones helped drainage and looked attractive. He learned this technique from working in the garden at home.

Deeper holes were used for shrubs and rosebushes because the roots were thick and long. The bushes challenged Brock but he managed an even layout throughout the flowerbed. He pricked his finger only once from a rose thorn. The tiny puncture stung until he focused on the chores at hand. His schedule repeated in the large flowerbeds along the back walkway.

"Lunch is ready. Come and get it." Mr. Challens called from the back door.

He enjoyed his favorite meal of leftover stew and homemade bread. The smell of steaming bread increased his appetite. He was hungrier than he thought.

"Are you in a hurry, son?"

"I haven't had a chance to repair much in the back yard, sir." Brock headed for the door.

The man put up his hand, halting him. "Take your time. There's no need to rush and please, don't call me sir. Mr. Challens sounds friendlier."

"Okay, Mr. Challens."

Brock raced outside to gather pieces of broken birdhouses. He salvaged the recyclable. He looked everywhere for parts. A hook outside the study window caught his attention. He thought of the perfect gift to hang from the window ledge.

The birdbath stand cracked down the center. He scrapped the plastic object and raked the back yard. He stored wood scraps inside the shed and organized tools in their proper place. Brock inspected the outside of the wooden building. Chipped wood splintered from the wall. He informed his boss of the problem. Brock stood like authority as he suggested, "Your shed will need more than paint to fix it. There are chunks taken out of the wood and paint won't cover up the damage."

"You might have a point, son. Tomorrow we'll take some measurements and see how much wood we need for repairs. Are you finished for today?"

"Done. Is there anything else you want me to do?"

Mr. Challens handed Brock a book. "Here is an interesting story to read. It's called, 'Holes' by Louis Sacher. You will find it quite appropriate to your recent encounters. Shortly after it was released, back in 1999, I read this when researching titles for my class. I found a winner. See what you think and I'll see you in the morning."

"Thank you. I'll get right on it." Brock dashed out the door, waving.

A frightful sight stopped Brock in his tracks. Eggs plastered the living room window of his house. Yellow globs smeared every inch of glass. Streaks ran between tiny chunks of shells. Broken eggshells scattered on the ground and sidewalk. Brock dropped his bike, racing for the hose. He soaked the slimy mess but water only greased the glass. He scurried around for a pail with warm sudsy water. A stepladder raised him high enough to wash the window. He scrubbed as fast as he could. His short fingernails scratched caked on egg yolk until it was removed. The window appeared cleaner. He covered up the vandalism in the nick of time. Dad returned from work not suspecting a thing.

Brock spent days looking over his shoulder after the egg mess at home. He realized his ringleader was on the loose and he worried about Justin's next prank.

Friday morning Brock rushed to work concerned about his new friend. Panic struck the second time around. He gasped at the sight hanging from a tree limb in the back yard. A cloth scarecrow attached to a pine tree branch. The black body tied by a thin rope. Arms and legs drooped and a noose wrapped around its neck. Red spots splattered down the chest with a splash around the throat.

"Oh, No!" Brock squealed.

He turned to the back door and another stuffed person hung from the hook outside the study window. A frantic search around the yard justified Justin's absence. Brock rushed to the backyard. He pulled out a jackknife and cut down the sick joke. He grabbed a ladder from the shed and placed it against the house. He climbed up and unhooked the second trademark. He scurried around putting the yard back in order. Brock washed his hands of the scarecrows dropping them into the garbage can.

The sick prank terrified him into a cold sweat when he remembered his friend. Brock reached the back door as Mr. Challens greeted him.

"I wondered where you were. One minute you're outside and then you're gone."

"You already saw them, didn't you?"

"Our visitor came during the night because I saw the scarecrows early this morning."

"They aren't scarecrows."

"What do you mean?"

"Those are puppets, dead puppets. I'm Justin's puppet and he wants me dead." Brock covered his mouth. A shiver ran chills up his spine as he realized what he had just said. Justin sought after him this time.

"Let's go inside." Mr. Challens extended his hand.

Brock calmed down and sipped his hot chocolate. The phone rang. The old man answered right away. He looked upset and spoke only a word or two. He placed the receiver back on its cradle.

The elderly man aged in seconds. Color faded from his face. Slender fingers rubbed his whiskers in a plucking fashion.

"What's the matter?"

The man took his seat. He gripped his cup with trembling hands. "Justin was released last week. His father picked him up early last Friday morning."

"I thought he would be kept in over the weekend." Danger enclosed with bad vibes circulating. "Something is wrong. What else did they say?"

"Don't mean to frighten you son but it appears that Justin showed the detention officer a gift he made. He was dropping it off for a friend when he left."

Strings pulled tighter than ever and Brock heard terror in the old mans voice. "The puppets, right? He was dropping off dead puppets for me."

"Yes. I should report this to the police." The old man managed to reach the phone.

"Wait! We know he's coming back because he warned us. I can't let him push me around and I won't let him frighten you anymore. This time I will stop Justin."

Tired and speechless, the old man sat in his chair. Mr. Challens changed from one day to the next. A contented and safe man yesterday was a terrified man today.

"Brock this is serious." Exhaustion silenced the man.

"Justin wants me for sending him to juvenile detention. His puppets made that quite clear. You rest for a while. I'll cut the grass and water everything first today. Make a list for the store and I can do the mail and groceries next."

The man grinned. "You're well organized today. It is nice seeing you take charge. I will have a shopping list ready when you are done."

The lawn mower roared around the small yard. A square cut ended in the center of the lawn. Brock finished the back yard and hooked up the sprinkler to the front. Water twirled in a light spray. The soft breeze floated cold droplets onto his arms. It dawned on Brock that he never went swimming all summer. He craved a quick dip as he watched drops hit the flowers. A sigh approved his outdoor maintenance.

"Ready for the shopping list." Brock washed up in the kitchen sink as his list was prepared.

Mr. Challens handed him twenty dollars and some

envelopes. "These letters go in the mail. I only need a few things at the grocery store."

Brock read the list:

"Bread, milk, butter, large eggs, and a bag of pretzels."

He shot a quick glance towards the old man. "Got it. If I'm not back in thirty minutes, come looking for me." A worried look crossed his friend's face. "I'm only kidding. I'll be back in fifteen minutes tops."

The Mini Plaza was minutes away and not busy. Shopping was great during weekdays. Brock cashed out at the teller within minutes and headed through the automatic doors. He stopped two doors down at the postal box and dropped the letters into the appropriate boxes. The heat seemed worse carrying the two grocery bags.

Spooked by a noise, Brock looked behind. A woman pushed a stroller on the other side of the street. The road was bare, otherwise. He slowed his pace listening to the sound. He stopped. The sound stopped. He walked faster and spun around.

A tall figure jumped into a nearby bush. His heart skipped a beat. Mr. Challen's driveway was a few meters away. Brock ran to the end of the yard and glanced back. No one was behind him. His rattled nerves fell to pieces over his leader's release. Something stuck out of the mailbox. Brock inched his way onto the front porch to retrieve a piece of paper. The stalker identified himself in the note:

Nice clean up job. Too bad it's for nothing.

Shouldn't leave your friend so long, anything can happen.

Remember, puppets are easily destroyed.

Brock crumpled the note in his hand. Measures turned desperate. Justin planned for revenge. He raced into the house not paying attention to the summersaults taking place in his stomach.

"Are you all right?"

The old man looked puzzled. "Shouldn't I be? You sound like you just finished a marathon."

"Just checking to make sure everything is fine. Got all the items you wanted. I'll put them away for you." Brock blurted out in a single breath.

He hurried around the kitchen placing groceries in the cupboard and refrigerator. He remembered his gift for Mr. Challens. He brought the bag in from beside the back step and handed it to his new friend. "This is something I thought you might like."

Mr. Challens pulled out the feeder. His dark brown eyes opened wide. They softened with wetness. "Did you make this, Brock?"

"Yes, do you like it? I worked at nights so I could finish it before my sentencing was done here. It's an 'all purpose' feeder."

"It's unique and very well crafted. The detailed work must have taken time to apply. Did your grandfather show you how to build this?"

"He used to make them years ago. I found one of his blueprints and tried it. If you use mixed seed you'll have Sparrows, Chickadees, and Finches flying around."

The old man examined the craftsmanship. "I used plywood for the houses and feeders I made. It is cheaper wood but if protected properly will withstand many years. This is the greatest gift in the world."

"I didn't know you made birdhouses. Maybe we can build one together sometime."

Mr. Challens set the feeder onto the counter. "Sounds like a plan. Where is the best place for my new bird feeder? Some place where I will see my little friends feed."

"I thought your study window would be a good spot. That way you could watch the birds while you worked at your desk. There is a hook outside the window but I think the feeder would be safer nailed to the window frame."

"You're really making wise decisions the past while. You're full of surprises." Mr. Challens inspected the feeder again. "The safest way would be screwing a block of wood into the cement bricks and nailing the feeder to the wood. It would be more secure than the window frame."

"That makes sense unless you prefer to hang it off the carport. It can be nailed into the siding and we don't have to bother with bricks."

"I prefer the feeder out my study window. There is more sun and it is a great spot to watch."

"What shall I do now?"

"Work is all done for today. Do you play cards, Brock?"

"Sometimes. I used to play Rummy 500 with my grandpa."

"That's my game. How about freshening our skills and opening that bag of pretzels for a snack."

Cards shuffled and the game began. Silence passed with concentration. The old man was good. Brock tried different approaches but lost every time.

"I lost again."

"Now Brock, it's only a game of chance. Cards are a fun and leisure activity. Gives your brain a different kind of workout."

"You sound like my grandpa. He always won and told me it was only fun, nothing to get upset over. The more you play, the better you get at it."

"That's true with life in general. The harder you work at something, the easier it is to do. Look at your reading," explained Mr. Challens.

His reading had improved the past few weeks. He read newspaper articles never tackled before and finished a complete novel in a week. "You're right. My reading is better and writing up lists to do each day has improved my spelling. I owe it all to you, Mr. Challens."

A pale face flushed as the aging gentleman shied away. "You did the work all by yourself. You can achieve whatever you set your mind to. It takes ambition and hard work, which you have proven to possess."

Brock checked the kitchen clock. He shuffled and played with the deck of cards in front of him. He observed the man across the table. His fingers fumbled and the cards flew over the table. The quiet atmosphere weighed heavy in his gut.

"I guess it's quitting time. Don't want you late for dinner or I'll be responsible for your next punishment."

Brock prolonged his visit. He looked around the kitchen trying to think of something fast.

"Are you positive there isn't anything else to do before I leave?"

"Nothing comes to mind. Go ahead, I'll be fine." The man smiled.

Brock got as far as the door and couldn't move. His hand stuck to the doorknob like a magnet. "You have my phone number if anything happens. Call me and I'll be here in minutes. Alright!"

His friend nodded and dark eyes swelled with affection.

"I mean it. If you need me any time of the night, I'll be here in a flash. I'm not leaving until you promise to phone me."

The man sniffed back tears and hugged Brock. "You are a dear boy. I don't know what I'd do without you. Yes, I will call if anything happens, now go on home."

12

STRINGS ARE CUT

Saturday morning brought an early visitor to 128 Sandy Road. Two delivery people handed out weekend flyers as they passed Brock. He accepted one for Mr. Challens. Mail poked out of the mailbox. Intuition warned him to check the contents before his friend did. His fingers paused as he pulled out the paper. A strange vibration made him twinge. Another trademark left by Justin Galley. The note read:

I could have gotten rid of him while you were gone.
Or did I?

The front door squeaked. A humped figure peeked outside.

The note slid into the back of Brock's shorts. "You scared me."

"Sorry. The mailbox rattled and I came to see what surprises were left."

If he only knew what surprises, thought Brock. He handed over the flyer. "You're in luck. I checked it before ringing your buzzer. Did you hear the mailbox just before you came to check it?"

The man twisted his mouth and squinted his eyes. "I came to

the door as soon as I heard the noise. I'm somewhat stiff this morning so maybe it took me a couple of minutes." Mr. Challens waved him inside.

Brock pulled his shirt down over the paper. He pressed to secure the note inside his waist band.

Mr. Challens handed Brock his usual morning drink. "Didn't expect to see you on the weekend. I won't have enough work if you start coming on Saturday's too." The man laughed.

The note bothered Brock. The delivery occurred the same time he rode up Sandy Road but no one else was on the street.

"Brock! Come back to earth boy." The old man waved his hands.

"I popped in to see if you wanted that bird feeder hung. Might as well use it now."

Mr. Challens sipped his coffee and nibbled on a piece of toast. "You've done an excellent job this month. The flowerbeds are great and quite imaginative. They won't last long with cold weather coming but they brighten up the place."

His friend picked at his breakfast. He wasn't his cheerful self. He looked depressed and the tone of his voice was quiet. "Is something bothering you Mr. Challens? You look like you just lost your best friend."

"Time is almost up, Brock. Next week is Labor Day weekend and school starts the following Tuesday. I guess you could say I am losing a good friend."

"Are you saying my work is done?" Brock became defensive. "You don't need me anymore. I can still come after school starts." A chapter of his life closed. It was like someone shut the book on his life and an empty spot grew in the pit of his stomach. Brock wasn't ready to say goodbye. He sprung from his seat wrapping his arms around his new friend.

Mr. Challens choked on his toast. He washed dry crumbs

down with coffee. "Whatever gave you the idea that I didn't need help around here? You can still work for me."

Brock let go clapping his hands in joy. "I thought you were saying goodbye the way you were carrying on." He danced around the tiled floor in circles. He caught his breath long enough to confirm what he heard. "My work isn't finished and I can keep the job, right?"

The old man laughed. "Brock you are some character. Yes, you have a permanent job for the weekends. I couldn't imagine hiring anyone else."

"The yard does look pretty good and the company is not bad, so I guess we're stuck with each other." Brock winked at the old man. He calmed down for a second and added, "I'll have to find out if Mr. Wilson still wants me part-time at the garage. I have to organize a schedule for my birdhouse business and school work."

"Take a breather, son. You have had your share of making decisions. Sounds like you need a partner. Maybe there is someone interested in making extra money on the weekends."

"Trenton. He likes outdoor work. I can bring him to visit when he gets home."

"That's settled. Now let's take a look at my new feeder."

Brock stood the ladder against the house. He removed the hook from the window-frame and nailed the feeder. Mr. Challens handed him a drill, which he made two holes into the concrete. It was hard but the cement bits were designed for this purpose. He placed a block of wood below the holes and marked a dot where the screws went in the wood. He drilled the wood and screwed it into the brick surface. Brock secured the feeder into the wooden piece.

He sat on the step beside Mr. Challens. "Looks good. Won't be long before the birds notice their new feeder and treats."

His friend smiled. "I agree, Brock. That's one handsome feeder."

"Is there anything else that needs done while I'm here?"

"You've done plenty. How's the new computer coming along?"

"I started typing from passages out of my go-kart magazine. I'm not sure about the keyboard, and my index finger is getting sore. I hope I will know some of the keys by next week."

Mr. Challens concentrated on the feeder. "Once you master the keys you'll be on your way. I guess I did hire that master of all trades, after all."

"I should go and practice before Dad gets home. See you Monday unless you need me before."

The old man waved Brock on his way.

He dashed down Sandy Road turning onto Mackey Avenue. Brock weaved onto gravel when a bike pulled out in front of him. He lost control and ended up in the ditch.

"What's the hurry Statler? You cut me off. You should have a driver's license for that thing," said the boy.

Brock yanked his bike out of the ditch when he recognized the voice. He looked up and down the street. They were alone. "What are you doing here, Justin?"

"Is that all you have to say after two weeks. I get locked up and there's no, how are you, or what was it like?"

"I didn't expect to see you, that's all."

Justin relaxed over his handlebars. He watched his puppet closely. "Why wouldn't you expect to see me? We never finished our last job."

Brock stared at the cold eyes. The zipper marks seemed longer and more visible. A hard beat pounded in his chest but he never moved. "The job was done. You hospitalized a senior citizen and paid for it. I am still paying for it."

"I forgot. You got to play housekeeper while I spent time locked up in a detention center with a bunch of loonies. That was a lousy deal if you ask me, Statler. Seems like you got off easy."

"You got what you deserved."

"Is that so. My puppet sounds too good for his leader all of a sudden. You make me sick, puppet." Justin dropped his bike and strutted towards Brock.

Terror consumed him. Silence froze time. Justin stopped a foot away from him. Brock jerked his head back from the warm air breathing down on him.

The leader poked his finger into Brock's face. "There is a way to fix all of that self-confidence you have developed."

"No way. I am not your puppet and you are not pushing me around anymore Justin Galley." Shocked by his own words, Brock waited for a reaction. Justin stood still. Minutes passed and no punch to the head, not a single movement. The big guy remained calm.

"You got my message at the old man's house the other day. You know the consequences for saying no to your leader. I've laid out a plan that will take care of the old man for the last time. You are going to participate whether you want to or not."

"No Justin. I'm not helping. You are on your own for this one." Brock hopped on his bike for a getaway.

Justin waved his hands. "Better listen to the details, puppet. You and the teacher are both involved in the ending if you don't cooperate."

The bike stopped. Another battle undefeated.

"Smart choice. I am going to fry the old man's house tomorrow. Everything on the property goes, including him if he's inside. You are responsible for getting the old guy out of the house at ten o'clock sharp."

"Why ten o'clock?"

"If you and the teacher aren't out of the house by that time you both go up in smoke. Does that answer your question?"

Perspire released with queasiness. Brock figured a payback was in store for him but never expected Justin to go after the old man again. He listened to a serious attack of revenge on his new friend. He exposed his new relationship with the man if he hesitated.

"You want me to make sure Mr. Challens is out of his home by ten o'clock sharp, tomorrow morning. Is that correct?"

"You get smarter by the minute puppet. Persuasion goes a long way, doesn't it?" Justin verified the information, grinning from ear to ear. "Don't bother trying anything stupid, Statler. I've checked out your house and it is quite flammable. It wouldn't take long disposing of the Statlers too, since I live close by."

Brock caved beneath the horror. It took everything from spilling his stomach right in public. He faced the worst nightmare of the summer. This time deadly plans involved his dad if he acted against the ringleader. Devious eyes embedded in his mind as Justin shot gravel on his departure.

Dad prepared dinner as Brock sneaked in the back door.

"Hi son. How was your day?" Dad faced him when he entered the kitchen. "What's the matter? You look like you seen a ghost."

Brock leaned against the fridge afraid of releasing his insides. He knew what happened but believing was another story. "Justin started his threats again."

Lines appeared on his father's forehead. "What did he do? Is Mr. Challens all right?"

"Mr. Challens is fine at the moment. Justin left me a reminder to do as he says, or else. I found two puppets hanging outside Mr. Challens house a week after Justin was released."

"We have to report this. That kid is crazy and might do something terrible." His father grabbed the phone.

Brock stopped his dad's hand. "No Dad! I'm going to straighten this mess out by myself. It is time I stood up to Justin and prove I'm not afraid of him."

Mr. Statler sat at the table. He slid his fingers through short black hair. "Has he bothered you ever since his release?"

Brock lied once again. No way was he telling his father who the next victim might be if he disobeyed Justin's instructions. "No Dad. Except for the hanging puppets, there haven't been any problems. It frightened Mr. Challens at the time but we decided to let Justin know he can't push us around. I can't back down this time. This puppet triangle has to end and I'm going to destroy it."

"What puppet triangle?"

"It's like I joined a triangle instead of the Night Hawks. I'm the puppet and Justin has pulled my strings since day one. Mr. Challens has been the victim all along but the puppet has been caught in the middle."

"Don't be surprised if this kid plans something else. I want you to call the police if anything happens while you're at Mr. Challens house. Brock, don't forget to call me at the first sign of trouble. Whatever you do, don't take any chances. Promise?" Dad waited for an answer.

"Yes, Dad."

Brock laid in bed that night, sorting out pieces of Justin's plan. He replayed the leaders instructions. He explained all details before the actual crime. That wasn't Justin's normal behavior. He played the conversation over in his mind dissecting every word. Brock jumped from his bed.

"He's not planning this tomorrow. It would be daylight.

Justin wants Mr. Challens in the house alone. He's setting fire tonight."

Brock raced for the kitchen phone. He dialed, counted four, five, and no answer. He dialed again and dropped the phone. He ran into the living room shouting, "I'm going to see Mr. Challens. There's no answer at his place."

"Slow down, Brock. Maybe he went out for a minute."

"No he didn't go anywhere."

"What's the matter, son?"

"I think Justin is there." Brock headed for the door.

"Wait, son. I'll call the police."

"Dad, give me one hour to make sure Mr. Challens is okay. If I don't call by then come and get me. We don't want police going over if Justin hasn't got there yet. Wait one hour!" Brock dashed into the night.

It was dangerous riding his bike in the dark without a light. He followed the dim streetlights dodging shadows in his path. He raced to the end of Sandy Road, slowing down at the second house from the corner. Quick action over ruled fear. He dashed over to the cedar hedges and searched the property as invisible as he could.

A faint kitchen light showed through the living room window. His friend was awake. Brock peered through the branches. He focused his eyes to the darkness and crept closer. A scuffled sound stopped him. He stuck his head out for a better look. Justin came around the corner of the house, crossing the front yard. He bent over with something in his hands. He stayed close to the house. Brock wasn't sure what his leader was doing. Justin came into view beneath the living room window.

Panic struck! A red, five-gallon gas can appeared in the dim light. Time was crucial. He tapped his thinking cap. Brock raced for the back yard. Blackness filled the grounds. A shadow moved inside the bedroom. He searched the ground for the white stones in the flowerbed. He grabbed some pebbles and threw them against the pane of glass.

The elderly man came to the window. Brock threw another pebble. The window raised and a rough voice mumbled, "What are…"

"Sh," Brock interrupted. He pointed a finger to wait. After a quick search around the house he continued, "You have to get out the back door. Justin is pouring gas to burn down your house."

The man grabbed his chest and disappeared from the window. Brock rushed to the front of the house sneaking across to the driveway. Justin stood under the carport with the gas can at his feet. He pulled a pack of matches from his pocket and opened it.

Brock jumped into the open. The ringleader held the matches in front of him. "Well, if it isn't my puppet. This is an unexpected visit. Did you have to tuck the old teacher in and read a bedtime story before retiring?" Justin laughed.

Brock watched the book of matches. "What are you doing here?"

"You know the plan. I decided to do the job solo. My puppet caused some doubts so I wanted to take care of the job in a proper manner."

Brock inched closer until Justin raised the matches to his chest and tore one off. A band squashed Brock's ribs. Fear and lack of time controlled his pleading.

"You don't want to do this Justin. Do you want to go back to detention for a longer time?" The match jerked in the leader's hand. "Let's go home, Justin."

The leader stretched his arm. "You don't think I'll do it, is that it? Just watch your new friend burn for the trouble he's caused."

"He isn't causing trouble. You already paid him back. You are making problems for yourself, Justin. You're sick. Can't you understand that you need help?"

Brock leaped at the large frame striking the match. He knocked Justin over the gas can. Liquid spilled onto the cement. Justin squirmed underneath. Brock grabbed the ringleader by his hands searching for the book of matches. He found a large clenched fist impossible to open. Brock flew across the pavement. Gas soaked pants and shirt smothered him. A foot pressed against his stomach preventing him from getting up.

Justin towered over his body stretching his scar into a wide grin. The shrieking laugh horrified Brock. "Here goes nothing, puppet."

"Don't strike it. Can't you smell the gas? We are both covered in it."

Evil roared from the ringleader's lungs. Brock froze at the stranger above him. The devil appeared in the flesh. "Is that what your afraid of? You should have thought about burning before playing hero, Statler."

Brock leaped at the two legs standing in front of him. He knocked Justin off balance. A right hook smacked Brock's head backwards. The blow connected with severe pain. Another punch caught him under the chin puncturing the skin with his front teeth. Warm liquid ran down the corner of his mouth.

Brock exploded with a forceful jab to the leader's head. Another shot hit between the shoulder blades. He punched again and again. A final strike ended with the sound of sirens. Red lights flashed from his side view. The distraction gave Justin an advantage. He flipped his puppet backwards over his back.

Brock banged into the small car behind him. Stars appeared from impact. Something yellow flickered a few feet away. His eyes focused on the bright glow dropping to the ground. The match ignited into a balloon of fire. Flames whooshed in both directions around the house. Brock managed to stand. He steadied his weight against the car and blocked out the pain in his head. Gas soaked clothing hinted a quick escape. The blaze caught the empty gas can tossing it into the parked car. Brock lost his balance.

A fire truck pulled alongside the curb and a police cruiser followed behind. Flames spread under the car within seconds. Brock jumped sideways avoiding contact. Smoke choked and limited his breathing. He covered his mouth and dashed for the open driveway. The fire burnt out of control.

Brock stumbled onto the cement. He watched in despair as flames crawled up both sides of the small vehicle. Any dirt on the car burnt to a crisp in seconds. Burning tires polluted the area with black smoke. Smoldering rubber gagged Brock. Inhaled smoke suffocated his lungs. He held his ribs as a flaming path surrounded the entire house. Old wood never had a chance. In minutes, flames destroyed the front porch leaving a black metal railing.

Firefighters raced the long hoses to the scene. Water gushed on connection and Brock received a taste of forceful spray. His wind cut off in a breathless moment. A police officer rushed to his side. "You okay son?"

Brock nodded. He pointed at the house gasping for air. "Justin. There."

The police officer yelled to the ambulance attendant, "Take him to the ambulance. Looks like the car is going to explode."

The attendant wrapped Brock in a blanket and moved him

away from the commotion.

"Is anyone in the house?" asked a police officer.

Brock tossed the blanket. "Mr. Challens. I don't know if he got out."

He raced for the house but an officer stopped him. "You can't go back there."

The officer pointed to the attendant. "Take him with you."

"My friend is in the house. You have to get him out. He's going to have another heart attack." Tears rolled down his face and he cried harder. Blurred vision concentrated on the smoke and flames extending from the home. Siding burnt like dried firewood.

Voices shouted. Firefighters fought the flaming car. One fireman yelled, "Run! It's going to blow." The men ran towards Brock.

A large ball of black fire whirled into the air. Thick dark smoke choked as it consumed the front yard. Brock coughed and rubbed his burning watery eyes. The cloud moved his way. The explosion frightened everyone. Terrified neighbors ran for the road. The firemen challenged wide sweeping flames.

Shouting came from the distance. Brock looked for movement around the property. Two uniformed officers appeared from the other side of the cedar hedge. The men struggled with someone. Brock recognized the ringleader as he came into the light.

Justin dragged between the two large men. Hands secured with cuffs behind his back prevented a getaway. He yelled and kicked his way across the yard. He spit at Brock. "You'll pay, puppet. I'll get you big for taking sides with the teacher. I'm not done with you by a long-shot."

Brock ignored the threats. An officer shoved Justin into the back seat of the white police cruiser. The ringleader of the

Night Hawk's spoke his last words. "I won't be locked up forever, Statler. I'm coming to get you."

The tall officer slammed the car door and brushed his hands. Brock washed his hands of Justin, too. Relieved at his ex-leader's capture all tension and fear of the past two months sat in the back of the police cruiser. Brock's new friend was safe as soon as they found him. Disappointment settled over his friend's house. He covered the endless flow of tears and prayed for good news.

A female officer sat beside Brock on the curb. She wrapped her slender arm around him, releasing a soft voice, "Brock, is it?"

He nodded.

"We haven't found Mr. Challens anywhere. The officers are checking the property again. We didn't find anyone inside the house. We are searching nearby homes in case he went for help at one of the neighbor's."

"You didn't see anyone inside the house?"

"We went in through the back door and checked all the rooms. The house is empty."

Brock smiled. "That means he is alive." He jumped off the curb with a boost of energy. "That's good news." He glanced around expecting to see the elderly man walk out from the hedges. Anticipation mounted knowing his friend escaped the fire. In a flash, all excitement vanished. A disturbing thought entered his mind. "When I saw him at the window he grabbed his chest. Maybe he took a heart attack. I have to find him." Brock turned away from the officer.

She placed her hand on his arm. "We are aware of that, Brock. The paramedics will take care of him, so don't you worry. We will keep searching until we find your friend." She hugged Brock.

Firefighters fought the blazing fire for over an hour. Brock's patience wore thin. He searched up and down the street from his curb. He viewed movement from all homes at the end of Sandy Road.

The blanket wrapped around him served no comfort. Smoke lingered on the blanket, his clothes, everything. The smell was sickening. The night grew hotter from the fire. Brock perspired from either fire or nerves. Shock set in and scary thoughts crossed his mind.

He prayed for guidance, *"Please give me a sign. Tell me my friend is alive. I can't lose him too, Grandpa."*

Brock wobbled over to the ambulance attendant. His body trembled inside the blanket. "Has anyone found Mr. Challens yet? It has been hours."

"No word of him yet. It's only ten-thirty and time seems longer when we wait for news," said the attendant.

Two officers approached from behind. The attendant lowered his head. Brock met disappointed faces. He peeked around the officers and realized no one was there. "Where is he? Where is Mr. Challens?"

A young man answered, "Brock, we haven't found him yet. None of the neighbors have seen him. I'm sorry."

Brock listened but didn't understand. He was hysterical. "You're sorry for what? You haven't looked. He's around here somewhere."

The policewoman took Brock by the shoulders to console him. "Listen to me. Screaming and yelling won't find your friend. We aren't finished looking but right now, it doesn't look promising. Maybe we should call your father to come get you or I can drive you home."

"I'm not leaving. I'm staying here until he comes back. He's frightened and doesn't know Justin is gone." Brock pulled away from the officer. He was dazed by the yard. "I am waiting here for Mr. Challens."

The three police officers exchanged looks. The policewoman ended the confusion.

"You rest for awhile Brock. This has been a traumatic experience for you. When the firemen are finished I will take you home, okay?"

"Okay."

Curled up in his blanket, Brock waited in a trance. Time passed and the firefighters finished cleaning up. A final inspection inside and out of the house was satisfactory. Firemen reported no injuries.

Brock knew Mr. Challens was out there somewhere. A noise from the hedges brought him back to reality. He squinted but saw nothing. Moments later the branches rustled. Afraid of the outcome but anxious for his friend's safety drew him to the shrubs. Brock shivered as he sneaked around the end of the hedges. He peaked into the shadows with his chest heaving, non-stop.

A black Labrador pup chewed on something. He bent down retrieving a slipper. It was Mr. Challens plaid rubber soled slipper. Joy escaped his lungs.

"I found something," he shouted.

Brock uncovered a missing clue that led him on his own investigation. His sign came at the last moment.

13

THE TRIANGLE TRANSFORMS

Adrenaline pumped. Brock shouted, "I found a slipper." He was gone in a flash.

Police officers ended a group discussion without notice. The news alerted the ambulance driver and attendant. Action picked up scattering feet.

A voice shouted, "Go get him. We don't want to lose another person."

Brock followed the hedges to the back yard. A steady pace continued into the enclosed area. A thorough search warranted a check over every inch of ground. He found nothing around the wooden shed. His rhythm covered the property next to the house and beside the overgrown pine trees. His heart raced. Tension increased a tight band around his chest. Every green blade scraped his worn joggers. Brock felt each bump, pine needle, and hole that existed. He investigated every square foot of the property. Anxiety suffocated his ribs. The thinning air closed in and pressure deepened.

A picket fence crossed the back yard. Brock dragged his feet over uneven landscape. He reached the cedar hedge and worked his way back to the road. Terror and anticipation multiplied. His concentration accelerated.

A spot opened up a few meters from the back fence. He squeezed through a clearing and came out on the opposite side of the cedars. He took a deep breath positioning his direction for the road and proceeded with caution. Each step swiped right and left in front of him. A headache developed from the serious manhunt. Brock refused to overlook anything in his path. He rubbed his dried eyes. The burning remained but focus was necessary. He examined everything he touched. One hand directed his route as he contacted the pointed edging of the cedar branches.

Something growled and he tripped. He scraped his knees on the hard ground causing a stinging sensation. His scratches never slowed him down. The black puppy returned for a play session.

"Not now. Go away." Brock scooted the dog off but he wouldn't leave. He crawled on the ground reaching from side to side with his hands. The pup dragged behind biting his pant leg in play.

Brock stood and shook the animal loose. He moved quickly to escape the dog when he thumped his toe. He took two steps back. Crouched on his hands and knees he felt over the ground. The puppy bit at his fingers and barked. He swatted at the dog. "Get out of here."

Brock touched a piece of material. He discovered a slipper a few inches away. He screamed! "Over here. He's behind the hedges." The black Labrador retriever licked his face and sniffed at the slipper. Brock rubbed the dog's head and hugged him. "You knew he was here all along, didn't you boy?" His eyes watered with tears.

Static sounded from police radios. Voices cut in and out as

the officers closed in. Thumping feet vibrated the ground. Flashlights beamed through the yard. Branches cracked as officers shoved through the narrow opening and appeared on the spot.

Bright beams displayed a body. Silence replaced the sounds of turmoil. An old man faced down on the ground. A brown housecoat covered most of his body. Blue pant legs and bare feet exposed from the man lying on the damp ground.

Brock bent over the body and shook his friend's arm. "Mr. Challens are you alright?" No response. His body felt warm but his clothing was wet from dampness. Helpless and terrified, Brock touched his friend to wake him up. His clouded sore eyes impaired his vision. He was too late to save his friend. Heartache enveloped his aching body and nothing stopped the pain.

An officer squatted beside Brock. He turned the man over easy. The officer felt for a pulse, looked in his eyes, and shone the flashlight over the body.

"Is he still alive?" yelled Brock. His stomach moved into his rib cage pushing up to his chest cavity. The fear of death enveloped his whole body.

The officer waved his hand. "Get paramedics over here. He's unconscious."

Brock fell onto the ground hugging a torn slipper. All emotions drained from his body. He held an aging hand in the safety of his lap and caressed with a gentle touch. The day his grandfather died haunted him. Feelings swelled within and he looked into the sky.

"Grandpa please don't take him. He is just like you. I can't bear losing you twice. Please let him stay with me a little longer."

Paramedics rushed onto the scene bringing a stretcher. They

checked his vitals and placed Mr. Challens onto the flat bed. Brock held the old man's hand and stayed close beside the stretcher as they hurried to the ambulance.

"Is he going to be alright?" asked Brock.

"He will be fine. There is a bad bump on his head requiring attention. The scratches on his face are not serious."

Brock looked at drooping eyes watching him. A long tail wagged beside him wanting attention. He bent over and hugged the dog with all his strength. "If it wasn't for this pup I wouldn't have found him." Eyes watered with joy.

"Brock!"

"Mr. Challens, I'm so glad you're alive. Are you okay?"

A worn out old man wearing tattered clothing rested on the white sheet. He was pale and exhausted.

"I'm in one piece." The man moved and groaned. "I guess I twisted my ankle."

Brock grabbed the frail slender hand. He smiled and cried at the same time. "I thought you took a heart attack and died somewhere. Police spent over an hour looking for you."

"My chest tightened and I hurried to get out of the house. I brushed against something on the back porch. The next thing I knew I was knocked over." Mr. Challens sat up on the stretcher and moaned. He grabbed his head. "Must be a battle going on inside my head."

Brock examined the man's head. "You have quite an egg sprouting. You said something pushed you off balance? Was it Justin?"

"I don't know, it happened so fast. After I fell off the porch, my ankle was sore. I dragged my leg to get away from the house. I couldn't put any pressure on it so I headed straight for the cedars to hide. I went through some trees."

"I found you on the other side of the cedars. That bump on

your head must have made you pass out because you were unconscious when paramedics reached you."

Brock sniffed. He leaned closer to his friend and sniffed again. "Smells like you were in contact with Justin. There is gas on your housecoat."

"Where is Justin?"

"He's been caught, handcuffed, and taken away. I'm afraid it was too late though. Your house is a mess and extensive fire damage this time."

The old man peeked around Brock. His lower lip quivered and all expression faded. The remains of Mr. Challens home were death itself. Burnt wood and siding scattered the ground, new flowers were saturated, and scarred bricks remained from the flames.

A demolished car replaced the red pinto. The old man covered his mouth. "He burnt my Lizzy."

"Spilled gas spread the fire under the car. An oil leakage caught fire and the gas tank blew. The firemen tried to save it."

"Your work is never done, is it?" Mr. Challens patted Brock's hand.

"Don't worry! I have a few days before school to get a jumpstart on the cleanup. I will have this place like new in no time. Maybe make some improvements at the same time." winked Brock.

"Nice to see you still have a sense of humor after all that has happened. Did Justin put up much of a fight for the police?"

"He tried but he had no chance against law enforcement. I guess you can say he finally met his match."

"Looking at those cuts on your face and that shiner, Justin met his match earlier this evening."

"No big deal. He made me so furious I couldn't back down. Nothing else mattered except saving you from that fire."

"My guardian saved the day by guiding me to safety."

"That reminds me. I think I know what you meant by constructive guidance."

Creases formed around Mr. Challens mouth.

"You advised me about Justin through all the talks we had. You told me stuff that I wouldn't have listened to any other way. Everything you said helped me deal with my problems and how to face Justin. I made some tough decisions in the past two months."

"Who ever called you stupid needs some constructive guidance of their own."

"I think he's on his way to some guidance as we speak."

"I guess we don't have to worry about Justin anymore. Looks like the puppeteer has been captured and freedom has sprung."

Brock cocked his head in surprise. "I have had lots of time to think and I've realized that we have been involved in a triangle since the day I joined the Night Hawks."

"How did you figure that out?" smiled the man.

"I was Justin's puppet all summer. You were always his main victim. He invented a puppet to blame if his plans failed. I ended up the one pulled between his actions and trying to help you when Justin took revenge. The three of us were joined all the time."

The man squeezed Brock's hand. "You are a mature young lad. This has been one confusing and terrifying summer for all of us. I believe you have learned more than constructive guidance this past month."

An old half-ton truck sputtered into the driveway. Brock knew the blinding lights came from his dad's truck. The slim figure darted his way. He grabbed Brock in a tight embrace.

"You okay, son? I was all set to come and get you when the

phone rang. I was positive it was you calling, so I answered it. I got sidetracked but cleared up the situation."

"Everyone is safe now. Mr. Challens needs medical attention but he'll be home in the morning."

Dad looked around the yard and squeezed Brock. "What a mess! Did Justin do all this?"

"That's Justin for you. He shook up the whole neighborhood in the process. I hope Mr. Wilson isn't too anxious for me to work for him, Dad. Looks like I have a full-time job here." Brock pointed.

Dad grinned. "You never cease to amaze me, son. After the experience you've been through tonight and you still manage to be concerned about other people. You worry about your new friend and leave the boss to me, okay." Dad looked back at the truck. "I almost forgot. I picked up a hitchhiker on the way over."

A short figure stepped out of the passenger's seat. Red hair and glasses sparked memories. Brock thought he was seeing things.

"Trenton! You aren't supposed to be home until next weekend."

The heavyset boy raised a high-five to Brock. "A little bit of pleading goes a long way. My dad got tired of the begging so he picked me up this morning."

"Now I have both friends together." Brock introduced Trenton to Mr. Challens. He was proud having his dearest and closest friends at his side.

Mr. Statler nodded to the man on the stretcher. "It's nice to see you are alright. Thank goodness for neighbors."

"No, I give thanks for having my own guardian angel or I'd be history."

"Brock knew you were in danger tonight," said Mr. Statler.

"I am grateful for a persistent young fellow like your son. This is the second time he has saved my life." Glassy eyes appeared and pale skin changed to a darker shade of red.

"Now that's enough talk. I think the ambulance attendant is ready for his patient. He promised you would be out by morning. They want to make sure you only twisted your ankle, and they want to clean up those scratches. He doesn't see you having a concussion, but the doctor will examine your bump."

Two attendants lifted Mr. Challens into the ambulance. "Time for a ride, sir."

The old man lifted his head before the doors closed. "Explain to Trenton about his new job. Long hours and little pay." He held his head and whispered, "Looks like you have reconstructed your triangle, Brock." The man fell back to rest as the doors closed.

Brock waved to his modest friend. Mr. Challens offered much more than working experience. Long hours and little pay were minor compared to the life experiences he learned. He digested lessons of crime, loneliness and true friendship.

Confident strides sprung with each step as Brock headed for the freckle faced boy. The night brightened and hope restored.

An arm wrapped around Trenton's neck. "Have a proposition for you, buddy. A once in a lifetime learning experience you will never regret. Think of serving a jail term of hard labor with all the loving guidance and knowledge you can master!"

An eager smile broke free on the freckled face. The wheels of trust were put in motion. A new triangle formed with Brock and his best friends.

Printed in the United States
47669LVS00002B/128